I cut his throat and I slaughtered him just like an animal. It had been easier than I had ever imagined.

The knife, it glided through his poisonous, rotten flesh, again and again. All that time, he looked at me, pleading and begging. He was desperate for me to take his money, his car, his phone; but I wanted nothing from him.

He had done enough damage. Why would I want to possess any of his filth? His destruction is a rebirth. A cleansing. He is free no longer, and never again will he cause such hurt.

Night Duty – Six months later

"You're a bloody nightmare. Can't you just hold it?"

"Look Jen, I need a piss, and I can't go to another call until I've had one! Let me just go back in, I'll be five minutes tops!"

"We haven't got five minutes. We're already assigned; Misper Enquiry."

"I flipping hate silent assignments. What happened to being asked over the radio if you wanted to take the next call? Putting up for it, rather than just sending it down. We're not blinking robots. Urgh, Missing Persons Enquiries. What is it? Another bloody teenager who has got themselves pissed, and is late home? I take it you've already accepted?"

"Yes!" *The female officer replies chirpily, and in response the male officer sighs, clearly annoyed....*

"Well, I didn't realise that I was crewed with a toddler and he hadn't brought his potty!"

"Look it's early enough. No one is up yet. Let me quickly nip in here."

Parked up in a lay-by, the male officer exits the vehicle...

"I'll be back in a mo."

"519 Mike Delta from 298 Mike Delta receiving over?"

(What the hell does he want now? I'm not wiping his arse...)

"519 from 298 receiving..." *(radio silence).*

"Mike Delta from 298MD receiving" *(panic in his voice).*

"Yeah, go ahead 298."

"Um, I think I need CID here. I've found a body."

"What's your location 298 and do you need LAS?"

"In Bramley Wood, junction of A267."

"Ok received 298, do you need LAS?"

"Negative MD. It's too late for an ambulance."

"Shit, shit, shit!"

The adrenaline has already taken over. I thought he was just pissing about! I didn't think he actually needed my help... I exit the vehicle and make my way through the clearing and into the hedgerow. The street lighting instantly vanishes. Darkness engulfs me, and the presence of the September early morning mist, it makes it even more eerie. I can then just about make out Gary's form.

"Bloody hell, Jen! Why didn't you answer me?"
"I'm here now! What have you got your knickers in a twist about?"
"It's a flipping body Jen, and I've just pissed all over it!"

As she looks down, with her eyes now fully adjusted to the light, all she can see is the remains of a body. Its carcass covered in both mud and leaves, and next to it, is a puddle of Gary's steaming piss.

Forensic Examiner Jones

05:15 am. The red glow of the numbers burn my eyes as I look over at the time. It is too early for this. Why did I let her talk me into another bottle? Drinking wrecks me anyway, but on a school night! What was I thinking?

John is long gone. The warmth from his side of the bed disappeared at 04:30 am. I'm flying solo this morning and I have the mammoth task of getting the girls ready, and over to school by 08:00 am.

I lie there dry-mouthed, and I contemplate how I am going to get my heavy head up off this pillow without being sick. Then I hear it.... the shrill of my work mobile. My day has begun.

"Morning Shirlie, how's the head?"

"What do you want this early? I'm on kids' duty today. I'll be in later...."

"Later is no good for me, I need you now! A body in Bramley Wood."

"Shit, really? *(My stomach lurches).* Look give me an hour; I'll see what I can do."

I end the call, and the adrenalin has kicked in. I'm sweating but I know what I need to do.

"Kids quick! Get up! Mummy has got to get to work."

Josephine

24th February 1980 06:22 am

"Come on you can do it! I can see the head, it's out! Well done, Violet, you are doing so well…. That's it darling, pant, pant…. and with the last contraction, push, yes PUSH… That's it, well done! You've done it! You've got a perfect little daughter. Oh, Violet! You are a Mummy! You should be so proud of yourself. Look at what you've created. She's beautiful."

They whip her away from me. She's silent. Why is she silent? I think for a second that maybe all of my prayers have been answered, but then I hear her. An almighty scream and I know that they haven't. I'm still in this nightmare and I have no way out.

They put her on my chest and straight away her little mouth is nuzzling my nipple. Just like he did. Sucking and taking without asking. She's his daughter all right.

It must be a shift change, as I don't see the midwife who acted as blonde cheerleader throughout the birth. I now have this fat middle-aged woman with a grin from ear to ear. Her voice appears to be on the edge of bursting into song every time that she speaks. She's just like a plump Julie Andrews.

"Oh, that's fantastic, she knows exactly what to do. Breast is best! That's the best start you can give her. What a fantastic Mummy you are going to be."

She places a cup of tea, toast, and jam on the side, and tells me to eat it to get my strength up. She then goes on to say how lucky I am that I didn't rip, and that there will be no stitches for me. I suppose I'm meant to be pleased. I try to interact with a weak smile but I'm so tired, and all I feel is used and dirty. She takes the baby from me, and says she'll dress her whilst I have a shower if I like? She then asks me where my hospital bag is? I say I must have misplaced it.

The truth is, I don't have one. I'm not prepared.

Shelley

I didn't always know that I'd been adopted. Initially, I thought that I was just like any other kid.

Mum and Dad were wonderful. Just so incredibly supportive. I have the fondest memories of growing up. I remember this one time at Play School, and me being the hula girl from many lands. My mum had made me the perfect rainbow skirt out of crepe paper, and as the nativity went on, the boy who was sat next to me had removed every strip. After he had finished, I was sat there in just my pants. How Mum and Dad laughed about it, when they reminded me years later, saying...

"Oh Shelley, your face was a picture... if looks could kill, he'd have been stone dead!"

All I remember is the anger building up inside, and me not knowing what to do. Him taking something that wasn't his, and me helpless and unable to stop him.

I vividly remember my first year at school. In those days you joined in the term after your fifth birthday. I started in the February and oh boy, was that a harsh winter. Deep drifts of snow. Mum walked me down in the morning. Both of us slip-sliding on the non-existent gritted pavements. There was no health and safety provision in those days. No radio adverts spouting "Had an injury that's not your fault?" No, we just trudged on through.

I hated it when she left me. Tears welled up, and every time that she unpeeled my leg or arm from her, to pass me over to the teacher, I would immediately find another anchor point. That was, of course, until Mrs Lynham managed to break her free. I had no idea that my poor mum would go home crying; worried about the psychological impact of me being left again, and what long-term damage that would cause. In truth, however, by the time she had crossed the threshold of the school gates my tears had dried, and I was happily creating another painting, which I would proudly present to Dad and her later. Always the colours of the rainbow, that inevitably turned out to be a messy brown masterpiece once I'd finished.

I was oblivious to my very early beginnings. If I ever did feel alone at school, I would grab my scarf off of my yellow peg, which also held my PE kit, (contained in the bag which Mum, had cleverly made from an old pillowcase) and I'd nuzzle my face into it. It always smelt of Mum. Every morning you see, she would squirt a spray of Anais Anais on to it, so that it would smell of her. Mum was smart like that. She knew exactly how to protect me and make me feel safe. My scarf smelling like her, was as if she was with me; giving me a hug.

Just her perfumed scent gave me inner strength and comfort.

DCI Jo Gordon

Bramley Wood – 06:00 hours

"Right then, what have we got here?"

"Alright Ma'am, I found it. I've put a cordon in...."

"Yes, I can see that. Well done! I also hear that you marked the spot in a rather unique way." *DCI Jo Gordon raises an eyebrow whilst talking to PC Gary Fuller.*

"Yes, sorry about that Ma'am. I was desperate, and I just stumbled across it, him, um I'm not really sure what they are. They appear to be.... well, umm cremated?!"

"Ok, so have you checked the body for ID?"

"No Ma'am, there was nothing obvious and well I've never come across a sudden death like this before. Mine are usually sitting in a chair, or lying in a bed with the TV blaring. We only get called because the neighbour has noticed the mountain of post, or there is a strange smell... Obviously, I usually turn that type to check for foul play, but this is kind of obvious Ma'am. Being in the wood, covered in leaves and all. As far as

I'm aware this is not an ancient burial site. I don't think that the body has somehow got disturbed. Mind you, with all the rain we've had... I suppose the land could have eroded so badly that they've popped to the surface...." *PC Fuller rambles on and is cut off mid-flow by the DCI.*

"Right, thanks for that. Keep your theories to yourself for now, and next time, please try not to relieve yourself in a crime scene!"

"Yes, Ma'am. Sorry. Shall I mark you on the scene log?"

"Well, am I entering the scene?"

"Yes sorry. I'll make a note now."

"Fantastic! Well done. I'll get you relieved soon. Early Turn will be finishing their briefing, and I need this site secure before anyone else contaminates it!"

Scene Examiner Jones

I open the front door with one shoe on, trying to get the other on whilst hopping. My handbag and laptop bag are slung over one shoulder, with my coat hanging off the other. Clearly, I'm not looking my best. My dark hair is scraped up into a rough ponytail and I've touched up the remnants of last night's makeup. Although not to any great effect.

"Mum I really don't know how to thank you. Yes, John was already up and out. I know next door are at their Gite (*doing it up again before the Christmas period…. It's apparently a good earner over the holidays, people wanting to get away from it all...so they couldn't help*). Anyway, they are awake at least. Both are still in PJ's… Maggie is in the kitchen contemplating what concoction she wants for breakfast, and Heidi... Well, Heidi is awake. Good Luck!"

I shout this at the very last minute before the front door shuts, and I blip the car fob. It's like handing over a baton. With Mum now in charge, I make my escape.

I load up the car, before searching my handbag for my phone which contains a text from Jo, and the postcode of where I should have been an hour ago.

Sitting in the driver's seat and turning on the ignition, a wave of nausea overtakes me. *I can do this, I must do this, it's my job.* By way of deep breathing, I manage to make the urge to vomit subside, and I tap in the jumble of letters and numbers that my tired eyes are trying to decipher. Then in what feels like hours, the satnav jumps to attention telling me it's calculating my route, and "there are traffic disruptions ahead." Fan-Bloody-Tastic!

After a little over an hour, I have arrived. Police cars, officers, and blue and white billowing tape line the route. I park up, take a deep breath, and to my right, I at once sense someone. It's Jo. She taps on the car window. "So nice of you to join us. Shall we get to work?"

Suited up and ready to go, I follow Jo into the scene. It's cold and damp, even though we are only in mid-September. We were lucky enough to have an Indian Summer. I say lucky, as it only really lasted a week, and since then it's rained and rained. Although right this minute we appear to be having a respite, and I inspect the scene without the usual persistent drizzle that is nature's cleanser. Great for the circle of life; not so great for preserving evidence. In any case, none of that would really matter here. I instantly see that forensics are going to have their work cut out with this one. The body has clearly been burnt. It appears that the fingers have been severed. The bones are blunted, and the teeth are missing. Unless we find a little gem nestling in the dirt, supplying some form of ID, we are going to have to rely on missing person reports, a facial mock-up, and the general public to have any chance of ID'ing this one.

Jo comes up to me "So then Shirlie, what do you think?"
I reply wearily.
"Drinking on a school night is a shite idea."
"Yes love, for you maybe but I'm a pro! What about this mess, any ideas?"
"Not really. I can say male for now; just because of the body shape, height, etc. But other than that, nothing. I'll get my lot to bag him up and the scene processed, and then I'll come back to you."

DCI Jo Gordon

I've had a long telecon with the powers that be. All of them wanting to know how the investigation is progressing. I really do wonder what happens when you reach the higher echelons. Rather than let you do; they constantly chase you for reports that they haven't given you the time to complete. I dutifully (but through gritted teeth) tell them that I have my best people on it, and that I will update them as soon as I have something. However, what I really wanted to say was:

"Piss off you bunch of pen pushers! I'm busy doing the real police work here... I'll obviously give you an update when I have something to update you with!"

It does unfortunately come with the territory. Being good at your job and delivering, means that they get used to results. It's my own fault, they are like Pavlov's dogs, I've conditioned them!

I silently say a prayer *"Come on Shirlie, do your magic and get these idiots off my back!"*

My next telecon is in 4 hours, and the countdown has begun.

Scene Examiner Jones

I make my way back with the body, and I go straight into the lab. Jo is keen for a quick ID. She thinks that this will speed up the investigation, and get Management off her back. It gives her a starting point I guess, and from there she can identify the motive, suspect, etc., get me with the lingo... a year ago it was test sample this, decalcification that... She also wants cause of death "on the hurry up!" Her words, not mine. However, I opt for the former. Let me see if we can at least identify this male. That's what I want to know. Was the killer sufficiently forensically aware to cover their tracks? It certainly appears that way. The body had been burnt and their teeth removed. I wonder if they had factored in the warmer weather of the summer to have been the perfect time to have buried the body? Mother nature had given them a helping hand in getting away with their crime.

I text John to tell him that he needs to sort the girls out for the next 48 hours, and then I put my phone on silent. I need to concentrate on this. Taking a sample of bone powder, I get to work.

Scene Examiner Jones

I slept at the lab over the past two nights, working on the samples. John thankfully wasn't on-shift, and so he could have the girls. When I did eventually make it home, Mum was babysitting. She'd been trying to teach Maggie to knit, and Heidi had been helping. I say that of course, in the loosest of terms.

Apparently, John had been called into work, and Mum yet again, had stepped in at the last minute. Anyway, she was keen to get back to Dad, as he said he would cook the Sunday Lunch, but Mum wasn't happy with him doing it, preferring it done her own way. So, I kissed her on the cheek, and I watched her leave. Her perfume, it slightly lingered after closing the front door, taking me back to when I was small.

I called out to the girls, letting them know that I was home, and they had briefly popped their heads around the kitchen door. They excitedly told me about the movie night, they had had with Daddy the previous evening. He had allowed them to eat pizza in front of the TV. Heidi had an impish grin, whilst informing me that they had stayed up late, and that they had watched 'The Pirates of the Caribbean', and that it was a 12 (classification), and she's only 4! Bless her, she loves a bit of rule-breaking that one! They both rapidly lose interest in me and they disappear off to the playroom. They only pop back for a snack, when their tummies start to grumble, or when they think Mummy needs a little TLC.

I'm sat at the kitchen table with a glass of wine and my laptop open. I am trying to type up the report. My unwashed hair is also now a creation of bows, clips, and hair ties. Heidi has been playing hair stylists whilst I've been "working." I think she has missed her mummy over the last few days and nights; I know I have definitely missed both of them.

I have eight missed calls from Jo on my mobile, and I see from the display that that number is about to increase to number nine.

I feel like shit, and I can't seem to concentrate.

John comes home. I hear his key in the door before I see him. He looks shattered. He's been working on some firearms job. Although we work in the same sphere, we rarely discuss it; other than shifts and how we are going to cover the childcare. Overall, it works quite well; breakfast club, after school club, Mum, the neighbours, and of course the electronic babysitter (the TV). Which helpfully, has entertained the girls for the last hour, whilst I have been struggling to put something meaningful together.

"Hey, Baby," *he says wearily, glancing at the half bottle of wine next to me.*

"Any of that going spare? It's been a pig of a day."

"Yes, help yourself, in fact, take my glass. I have only had a sip. I really need a clear head for this. I just poured it out of habit."

He takes the glass and puts it to his lips; he then glances at the laptop screen.

"You been in long?"

"I have, and I have nothing to show for it, other than my new hairstyle; you like it? Heidi's creation. They are in the lounge by the way, watching the TV."

I sit looking at John as he smiles at me. Although he's tired, and he could definitely do with a freshen-up, I get a pang of love. Those kind eyes shining out through the creases in his face, and then panic sets in and another wave of nausea. *"What the hell am I doing?"*

John goes off to find the girls, and he then shouts back at me, "Baby, why don't you give up doing that for now, you never achieve anything once you've hit a block. It's nearly half seven. Why don't you go to a class? Clear your head, and then you can get back to it. I'll sort tea."

Snapping me out of my moment of anxiety, there it is again, that pang. *"God, what did I do to deserve him. He knows me better than I know myself."* I put the laptop on standby, and quickly I run up the stairs, and then I'm back down, now changed into my trainers and gym gear. Heading straight for the door, I think that a HIIT class is just the ticket. It will sort me right out, endorphins always do... "See you in an hour! Thank you!" I shout.

DCI Jo Gordon

I've got nothing, and the Upper Management want something. You don't just find a body in the wood, and then go off the grid for the weekend. The press is all over this. Someone has leaked that it's UN-IDENT and that worries me. There is someone's Partner, Mother, Father, Brother, Sister, Son, or Daughter going out of their mind with worry. Thinking that it's their missing loved one. The hope that they have clung to for months is extinguished, and I can't tell them a thing. 101 calls have increased tenfold.

I know it's Sunday evening, and we all have plans but this can't wait. Why is she not getting back to me? She's meant to be the expert in the field, the whole reason we hired her. It's why I hired her. I stuck my neck out and pushed for her, and she's giving me nothing!

Scene Examiner Jones

I make my way out of the class; sweating, and physically exhausted, but my head is clear. I'm pumped! I see another 6 missed calls from Jo.

I make the call.

"Oh finally! What happened to you? You can't still be hungover. In fact, don't tell me, let me guess... It's been a manic weekend with the girls. John's been working. Back-to-back birthday parties, homework, housework, shopping, blah, blah, blah... Am I right?"
A little taken aback by her tone and blatant sarcasm. I reply "Actually no, I've spent the last two nights at the lab, trying to identify your chap!"
A little sheepish in her reply "Oh right, sorry. So, have you?"

"Um no, and I haven't written my report yet, as my preliminary findings were well, somewhat limited. I'm going back to write that now."

"Why, where are you?"

"Um, I went to a class. I needed to clear my head."

"Jesus Chris, Shirl!" Jo bellows this down the phone. Clearly her earlier embarrassment, of thinking that I'd sat and done nothing this past two days, didn't last long... "This isn't academia anymore! This is the real world. You can't fanny about, writing your reports for this and that journal in your own sweet time! I've got Monroe on my back. He wants to know if we have an IDENT! You are the best in the field. I just need you to focus and provide me with some leads. Anything really!"

"Yes, I'm sorry, but that is the thing, the science hasn't told me anything of evidential use. The body is too severely burned, the DNA compromised. The problem is that the bone fragments were degraded, and the amplification of genetic markers were near on impossible to identify, and unfortunately, it also means that cross-contamination of DNA, like PC Fuller's addition, is making this less than straight forward. I have run my initial findings through the databases and got nothing. There were no teeth, so I can't go down the route of dental records, no implants, no nothing. There are more tests, but they take time, and I'm not entirely sure that they will help." I continue "I also need to run more detailed tests to provide the exact time of death. I can estimate 6-9 months but that's it. More work needs to be done back at the lab, but he's clearly been there some time. I thought I had more time; there is no golden hour on this one, surely?"

"Ok, yes sorry. I just thought you'd be able to pull the rabbit out of the hat. You've done it before, and I'm sure you can do it again!"

"Yes ok, leave it with me, I'll do the prelim report and get that sent over. I'll work on the rest tomorrow onwards... Look, I make no promises."
"Yes, sorry Hun. I didn't mean to rant. Just email it to me when you can."

Jo's name disappears from the screen as the call is cut and now, I'm sat in the driver's seat of the car. I'm cold; the sweat on my back has hit the cool air and has started to chill against the leather seat, as has unfortunately, my endorphin hit. I make my way home and back to the laptop.

Josephine

"Josie" is what my dad called me. Much less formal and much more loving. That's what he was; a loving man. Mum was the disciplinarian. Dad was the fun one. I think that's why it hit me so hard when he died. The love and affection were gone in an instant, and Mum the practical and organised, ordered parent was left behind. There was no grey with her, just black and white.

Mum turned wholly to the Church after Dad. She'd always been Catholic. Dad was COE, although not that you would have ever known it. He loosely practiced, and that was usually from a bar stool. That said, he was moralistic, hardworking and he gave me a solid foundation of right and wrong. He was a good man.

I remember my twelfth birthday. I'd asked for a plastic wall clock that looked like the fob watch, that the White

Rabbit had in Lewis Carroll's 'Alice in Wonderland'. Dad had of course, bought it for me. I remember Mum, she had thought I would have been better with a more practical present; a body warmer, shoes or the like, but he had gone against her buying me the clock and then for some strange reason, he also bought me a diary.

I'd never wanted one, I didn't think my life was interesting enough to fill up the crisp white lined pages. Nevertheless, once I had it, I felt quite grown up and I loved it.

In my blue and pink mottled, faux leather 5-year diary, I would write everything that happened to me. My thoughts, desires, and ultimate heartbreak. I'd write it all down and then lock it up with the gold clasp, that held the pages, along with my memories secure.

Scene Examiner Jones

I finish the report, attach it to the message, and press send. It unfortunately, tells Jo nothing more than what I had already told her over the phone.

John has fed, bathed, and put the kids to bed. He's left the bath in for me, and I've just turned the hot tap on. I sit on the edge of the bath watching it fill. My mind is temporarily void of thought, and it feels wonderful.

John stands in the doorway.

"What are you thinking about?"
I turn to look at him, focusing on his dark silhouette against the landing light behind.
"Nothing actually, and it feels great."
"Did you get that report done?"

"I did, I've got more to do tomorrow, but at least I can relax for now. Jo was not happy with me; you should have heard her."

"Look, I know she's your mate, but you really should set some professional boundaries."

"I know, but she's stressed, and she worked hard to get me in."

"Yes, I know, and I am still not entirely sure why you joined. Academia suited you, us, so much more."

"John! Please, let's not go there. It's done now!"

"I'm just worried about you. You've changed so much over this past year. Stress doesn't suit you. You always look so anxious."

"Look, thanks for sorting the girls and tea. I'm having a bath, and then I'm going to bed. I've got a lot to do tomorrow."

John, clearly getting the hint, he turns and leaves. I then turn off the tap, undress, and sink into the bath; cleansing both my body and mind.

Josephine

I got into quite a routine. I'd have my tea, usually something along the lines of liver and bacon, cottage pie or toad-in-the-hole, etc. Mum was a traditional cook and she loaded the plate high and wide. Tea was always on the table by 6 pm sharp. This gave Dad the time to leave work at 5 pm, nip to the local for a quick pint, and then his tea would be steaming hot and, on the table, awaiting his return.

I'd wolf it down, have a bath, read my book and then I'd get my diary from its hidey-hole. I knew it had a clasp, but I liked the idea that it was also hidden, and out of view to any prying eyes. To be honest, it wasn't the most imaginative of hiding places at the back of the radiator, but for a naive twelve-year-old, it was the best that I could do.

Every entry started the same. "Dear Diary" and then I would list all of the non-eventful things that had happened to me that day, including what I ate for breakfast, dinner, and tea. It was like my very own Facebook, minus the likes or emojis, but still the same inane entries that people like to post these days.

Sundays, were probably my favourite day; not because Dad, rather than make me go to Church would take me to the play park (with of course the slight detour to the Pub on the way home), and not because Mum, having returned from Church would have prepared a magnificent roast dinner. No, none of these things. I loved Sundays because without fail, we would always eat delicious homemade cheese scones with butter and strawberry jam on them for tea, whilst we played scrabble. Just us, and not a care in the world, well other than me trying to beat Dad with a triple word score! This was the one day in the week, that we would relax in the front room (in front of the fire in winter), and have family time. It was fantastic. It would then get to 7 o'clock. Mum like clockwork would then say, "Right... School in the morning! Someone needs a bath and bed." I'd of course be obliging, and after my steaming bath, I'd put on my snuggly pyjamas, and then come down and give them both a kiss, before heading back up the stairs to bed. I always read a couple of chapters of whatever book I was in the process of devouring, and then I'd fill the crisp white lined pages of my diary with my thoughts of the day. Once finished, I'd make sure I put it back in its hidey-hole, snuggle down in my bed, and switch off my bedside light. I was then ready to indulge in whatever fantasy I dreamed of that night.

DCI Jo Gordon

2 Years before the body was found

It had been absolute years since I had last seen Shirlie. It was a chance meeting in a coffee shop in the main town. I recognised her as soon as I saw those distinctive blue eyes. She'd lost the white-blonde hair, that had led to her nickname all those years ago at school. She was more like Pepsi these days, with her long dark locks. In fact, I do vaguely remember her dying her hair at the time of our GCSE's, but I left school soon after to go to college, and I didn't think that she would stick with it. We didn't see each other again after then. I was amazed that I still recognised her.

I think she must have stayed on into sixth form. I myself, couldn't wait to leave and move on to pastures new. Well, what I couldn't wait for, was to mix with some boys. An all-girls school has its benefits, but meeting members of the opposite sex is not one of them! I was just so desperate to grow up, and to sample the forbidden fruit. Looking back now, I don't know why I was so keen. What this job has taught me over the years, is that the majority of men are assholes, and are only really in it for themselves. Yes, even after all these years I am still single. There are many notches on my bedpost, but not one worthy enough of a regular place at my breakfast table, well... all of them, bar one.

Anyway, I was working in Sapphire (the Sexual Offences Unit) and I was a DI. I had worked my way up since joining at 18 years old. Not one of these fast-tracked idiots that you get these days. Those with a 25 at the start of their warrant number. No, mine has a 19 at the front. I'm proud to have served my time; earning my stripes and now stars.

At the time, I was trying to get enough evidence to pass the CPS' (Crown Prosecution Service) Threshold Test, on a historic rape case. We knew who the suspect was, and he of course was denying it. His party line was that he had never met the victim, let alone raped her. The victim had really been affected by the incident, and her cooperation in pursuing this to court was hanging by a single thread. She just could not cope with the stress of it anymore. She had only really come forward due to several counselling sessions, and the hope that he might be prosecuted, following on from all the press coverage surrounding Jimmy Saville. Although her case was totally unrelated.

Anyway, I got chatting with her over a Latte, and she was a doctor no less. A Research Fellow at the University, and a Specialist in Advanced DNA Techniques. She had letters after her name, as well as a countless number of papers that had been published. She obviously didn't tell me all this at the time, but I am a bloody good detective and a sixty-second Google search had told me all that I needed to know.

My victim had kept her teddy bear that she had had since she was a child. In one of the ABE video interviews (Achieving Best Evidence), she had mentioned, that the whole time that that monster had raped her, and forced her to do what she did, she focused on that little bear. She said that when he was finished, he leaned over, kissed her lips, and said "Remember it's our secret." As soon as he was gone, she grabbed that bear, and she sobbed into its soft brown fur, holding it tight into her naked little form. I didn't think of it initially. I had assumed that any evidence that 'Mr Bear' might have guarded, would have been long gone. However, on thinking about it further, I realised I was making the classic mistake of thinking that my victim's childhood in some way may have been aligned to my own. I thought Teddy would have had multiple trips to the washing machine, which of course, and now rather fortuitously, he had not!

Anyway, cutting a long story short, I seized that little bear as evidence, and I sent it down to our lab, and unfortunately, it was useless. The DNA was too degraded to get anything evidential from it.

Sitting at my desk, and thinking about what else I could do, I remembered Shirlie and her specialism being DNA. We had swapped business cards and although at the time, I had no real intention of catching up, I dialled the number. I had a vague hope that she could help, or at least pass me on to someone who could.

Shirlie was delivering a seminar at the time, so an assistant took the details of my call. Within the hour she had called me back. She said that the case had struck a chord, and if there was anything that she could do, she would.

Anyway, I took the bear to the University Lab myself. Five days passed and bingo! She did what no one else could. She proved that my victim was raped by that monster. His DNA had clung to that bear's fur for all those years. He did know her; he did do all those things. The Jury took under an hour to come to a guilty verdict. She was my golden girl, and I knew at once that I needed her on-board, full time.

Josephine

Aged fourteen and a half

I wish I'd thought of it before. As you know after Dad bought me my diary, I religiously documented every thought and deed. In fact, even more so after his passing; it brought me some form of release, and or comfort I suppose.

Dad died suddenly. No real explanation. Here one minute, gone the next.

One day, however, I came home and I found Mum crying at the kitchen table. This sight was not a new one. I'd gotten used to it since Dad... Along with the various ladies from the WI popping in with hot meals, so that we didn't starve as we "got over" our grief. This day however, it was different. This day there was Mum sat at the table with a book in front of her. I recognised it immediately. It was my blue and pink diary.

Mum said that she had found it on my bedroom floor, under my window ledge (beneath the radiator), and rather than just leave it there, she had opened it and read the last few entries. These entries were my private thoughts, and not for my mother to read and digest. They contained my thoughts, feelings, and raw grief. ...and my mother, rather than take it for what they were; just the ramblings of a grieving and hormonal teenager. Oh no! She over-reacted, screaming and shouting at me, telling me how selfish I was. "Have I not lost enough? Do you think I need to be punished further? Holy Mary, Mother of God!" Those words burned into me, and thereafter I wrote my diary in code.

I developed my own cipher. I'd learnt about it in school. We were learning about the Second World War, Bletchley, and the code breakers. I was fascinated. I also found a much better hiding place for my diary.

Never again would my mother have the temptation to read my innermost thoughts and overreact, as she always did. Or even if she did find it, I doubt she would have worked out the code.   My mother wasn't that way. Great at cooking and homemaking, but ciphers and code-cracking, no way! My secrets from now on would remain just that, a secret.

Shelley

I vividly remember the day that I found out. It was in the December, and not that far-off Christmas. We had a real Christmas tree, so the smell of pine was strong, especially as Mum had put it in the front room bay window, next to the radiator. Dad was out at work and I was on school holidays.

I was getting to that age, that I was questioning the validity of Father Christmas. A number of friends at school with older siblings, had said that he didn't exist, and that it was actually your Mum and Dad. Logically it made sense, but the fear that if you didn't believe, meant that you also got no presents was way too much. I had to know for sure.

Mum was in the kitchen baking, and she thought that I was in the front room, watching a Christmas film on our old Amstrad colour TV. I'd decided that with Dad out of the way and Mum busy, it was the perfect opportunity to prove my friends sadly right, or hopefully wrong; so, I went on the hunt for presents.

I sneaked up the stairs, my heart in my mouth and a twist in my stomach. I knew what I was about to do was wrong, but curiosity had gotten the better of me. I went into Mum and Dad's room, which normally was out of bounds unless one of them was in there, or it was in the dead of night, and I had needed comfort after a bad dream.

In I crept, and I went straight over to the wardrobe. Opening the doors, I saw several black sacks squashed at the back of their expansive wardrobe, but it wasn't those that had caught my eye. It was a blue and pink mottled book, with a gold clasp. It had looked like a book of spells. To a small girl, it looked magical and I was immediately drawn to it. I picked it up and started to inspect it.

Engrossed in my task, I hadn't heard my mum come up the stairs. She had come to look for me to lick the bowl from her baking, and when she had not found me downstairs, she had made her way up to the bedrooms. I was in her room, on my knees, looking as if I were praying at her wardrobe. The pretty book was in my lap.

"Now! What have you got there, young lady?"

Startled, I turned around, knowing that I was in the wrong, but when I looked at her face, I was a little confused. I'd expected her angry face, ready to tell me off for snooping, but she wasn't. She almost seemed scared... anxious maybe? "Mummy" I said, "What's this?"

My mum, who still had cake mix on her hands, wiped them on her apron, and taking a deep breath she then went over to sit on the bed. She beckoned me over to sit with her.

"Bring the book and the carrier bag next to it." I gestured towards a worn 'Woolworths' carrier bag. "Yes, that's right, that's the one."

There and then, my mother, who wasn't really my mother, explained that I was adopted. And that the pretty little book of blue and pink, with the gold clasp was the only link, the only history that I had of who I really was, and where I had come from.

All I had wanted to know was if Father Christmas were real, and whether the presents had come from him, or them. Instead, I found out that my whole life up to this point had been a lie. Mummy hugged me, and I remember her telling me that I had been the best present that she and Daddy had ever been given. And do you know what? I believed her.

Josephine

The train journey was long. I had initially managed to get into an unoccupied carriage, and for the majority of the journey I was alone.

The baby had stayed quiet miraculously, but I had felt her begin to fidget under my coat, so I got up to see if I could find the toilet. I opened the wooden toilet door and I slid through the gap; the door sprung immediately shut behind me, making me jump. As I then slid the bolt across, the baby started to scream. I didn't know what to do, but I thought it had to be hunger, so I pulled my top up along with my bra, and clumsily, I tried to get the baby on to my nipple. The baby seemed possessed, and angrily tried to latch-on. After a few minutes, she had attached herself to me, and the rigid form that she had become, finally relaxed. As did I. I was able to put the toilet seat down and I sat on it whilst cradling her. The train's natural motion helped her to settle and we swayed side-to-side as we continued on with our journey. After about twenty minutes the baby was asleep, still occasionally suckling my nipple, so I managed to take her off, and luckily, she remained sleeping.

I remember, how frightened I was, she was so small, so delicate. I also remember congratulating myself inwardly, that I had gotten this far without any help. It was only when I felt a wet patch, that I realised that I needed to work out how to change a towelling nappy. I undressed her, and thankfully it was only a wee. I had to tackle the tar-coloured offering, which was presented to me later on in the journey.   All I can say is thank the Lord for "Johnson Baby Cloths!" The midwives had been very good, with their crash course in motherhood at the hospital, but it was still a daunting prospect doing it completely alone.

It was dark when we arrived at our destination. I hadn't really formulated any other plan than to take the baby somewhere safe, and then take all this pain away. I was finally going to be free, loved again, and back with my dad.

DCI Jo Gordon

I open the email on my work phone. I can't be doing waiting until I am back in the office. I scan it quickly, to see if she has included anything extra that will be of use. But no, nothing. It's exactly what she said on the phone, albeit with more technical jargon, explaining the processes undertaken, timings, etc.

It looks like to solve this one, I've got to go back to basics. I've already got officers doing house-to-house enquiries, to see if anyone remembers anything from 6-9 months ago. The problem now being that I don't have an exact timeframe, so it's difficult knowing if what you are asking is correct. What also makes this doubly hard, is that there are no neighbours close by. This really is the perfect spot for disposing of a body at. There is nothing here. The old church is now derelict and the wood that it backs on to is vast. It used to be used regularly in the 1970's to '80's. Apparently, the Youth

Group camped there, or so some of the older locals told me, but after the church was fire damaged, all that stopped. I'm surprised a developer hadn't snapped up the land; an absolute gold-mine. Well, it would have been prior to this grim discovery.

Josephine

Aged fifteen

I hadn't really planned to lie. But when I struggled sweating and in intense pain up to the A&E Desk, and I said that I was 'in labour', the first thing she asked me was my name.   I panicked and said "Violet." The woman behind the desk must have believed me, on the "in labour" part, as she straight away summoned a porter, and I was whisked up to the Delivery Suite in a wheelchair.

I was examined almost immediately and the Midwife said, "Oh dearie, haven't you done well, 9 cm's already. We'll have your baby out before you know it!"

The curtain was then swiftly pulled around the bed, and the stage was set.

They asked me lots of questions after the birth and I was settled in the ward. I say settled, it was hardly relaxing, more like a busy train station. Lots of comings and goings, and the noise! Babies crying, mothers snoring, tea trolleys, and the visitors; so many visitors. Proud grandmothers, each holding their own child's new-born. Older siblings, being bribed into accepting their new brother or sister, by receiving the gift of a new train or a new dolly. They never even questioned how the baby had miraculously been out and purchased their present, even though it was less than a day old!

I had no such experience. No one came to visit me. No one even knew that I was there, even the midwives thought that I was called Violet, and that was the story that I stuck with.

I gave them my full name, date of birth, and address. All made up of course, but closely related to fact, so not to raise any suspicion. I at least gave a date of birth that made me 19 years old, and not the 15-year-old that I actually was. The address was easy. I said that I had just moved to the area with my boyfriend. Not technically a lie; the boyfriend bit yes, but I had temporarily moved to the area, to a damp guest house on Queen Street. I made up a story that we had moved away to start a new life, as my parents didn't approve of my pregnancy.

"Barnaby," my boyfriend had just started an apprenticeship at one of the new build sites, which was why he wasn't with me at the birth. It was also why I hadn't called him, as I didn't have a telephone number for the site... I made excuse after excuse, but mainly he wasn't with me, as he didn't exist. I was completely and utterly alone in this.

The midwife, a smiley and jovial woman laughed at this... "Well, what a surprise to come home to!" I smiled weakly and said, "Yes, it's definitely something for us to get used to." After the midwife had taken all of my details, she advised that once the baby had passed a stool, we would be free to go home, and my boyfriend could meet his daughter. There was the option of staying a few days, to get used to things, but I declined saying that he would be worried as to where I was.

She asked me if my hospital bag had been found yet? I informed her that the last time I had it, was at A&E. She muttered…. "They'll take anything these days, if it's not nailed down!" And then she said, "Don't worry love, I'll get you sorted."

She certainly lived up to her word, as within the hour, I had a string bag stocked with nappies, a hat, a baby grow, and a sample pack of 'Johnson Baby Wash Cloths.' "In place of cotton wool," She explained to me. I'd never seen them before, and I was sure they would help with keeping the baby clean. Although, I wasn't planning to find out how effective they were myself.

I had made my plan. I knew what path I was going to take.

I left the hospital, and I held the baby close to my body. She was hidden under my coat. I did this instinctively to keep her warm, but also so that no one saw her, or took any notice of me.   I wanted to be invisible.

I walked briskly for the ten minutes it took to get to the rail station.   I was exhausted, but I knew I needed to move on as soon as I could. It was the only way.

Shelley

My mum, the Mum that I had always known was amazing. She slowly explained to me what being adopted meant, and how I had come to be her and Dad's little girl. She showed me the diary that had piqued my interest originally, and said that it was mine, and that I could read it when I was a little older. I could then learn more about who I was.

She also showed me the newspaper cuttings, of when I was originally left at the Public House. It was a strange place, I later came to think to leave a baby, but its name was 'The Inn', so maybe it had some religious meaning to her.

There had been a nationwide press appeal to try and find my mother, and reunite me with her, but it had been fruitless. There were no leads other than a midwife that had come forward. She said she recognised the string bag and the sleepsuit that I had been left with. However, the name and address that had been provided at the hospital was believed to be false, and it led no further.

I didn't know my mother's name. The diary's first page had been ripped out, done I expect, for that very reason, to keep me or anyone else from knowing her true identity. The only thing she did leave, was a jumper that I was wrapped in, along with a string bag containing a single towelling nappy, a sleep-suit, and this diary. One of the back pages had also been ripped out, and a note scribbled on it, stating that I should be adopted and cared for, as she could not do it herself.

John

When I first met her, I had absolutely no idea just how complicated my wife was. To me she was just this dark-haired beauty, who had happened to earwig a conversation on a train. A drunken conversation, I might add, that I was having with my mates. I can't really remember the detail, but she made a comment and that was it. I had captured her interest, and I talked to her the rest of the journey home.

Actually, I Interviewed her. I found out as the train gently swayed from side-to-side, that she was a few years younger than me, and that she had recently moved jobs. She had been given the opportunity to complete a PhD at the University. I also learnt that we were destined to meet. Our paths had crossed so many times before. We had attended the same Northern University as Undergrads. Although there was a two-year crossover period, and we were based at different campuses in the day, but at night, we would have been in the same Student Union Bar. Wednesdays, the Sports Team's traditional blowout night, we would have wound up in the same curry house, in an attempt to sober up before heading home, (well in her case.) In mine however, it was so that I had more stamina to go to the local night club and party-on into the early hours. We even went to the same gym up there.

I could not believe that this was the first time that we had actually met, given all of our previous opportunities for a chance encounter.

My station was quickly approaching as the driver had already announced the next stop, and so, I bravely with the help of the numerous Stellas', that I had consumed that night asked her if she wanted my number? Her face was a picture as she screwed it up, stating that she didn't take strange boy's numbers. Gutted, I turned to my mates with a look of despair. One of them piped up,

I can't remember who, "Oh go on take his number! He's actually one of the good ones."

The train slowed, and I thought that was it. She wasn't going to take it. But then she said in a slightly drunken and husky voice "You can take mine though." I didn't hesitate for a second, nor did I question her logic, as I pulled out my Nokia and plugged the 11 digits in.

The train had stopped at this point, and my mates were shouting at me to get off the train, but I managed to text…

I'll call you tomorrow x

And I was so grateful to hear the delivery tone chirp from her phone, confirming that she had given me the right number.

CJ

My initials, since forever have been CJ. I had been born to an alcoholic mother and a drug-using father. I believe that I was with them both very briefly, well, until the Social Services were tipped off by a concerned neighbour. I was then removed into care. I am not really sure what happened thereafter, as I wasn't adopted straight away, instead I was in the care system and went from one foster home to another. I also spent some time in a residential boy's home, which I vaguely remember as not being a very nice place to be. The older boys ran it, and the staff turned a blind eye to the beatings, as the pecking order was fought amongst its residents.

All I remember is that before that date, my life had been hard. I was unloved, a burden and I had no one, or nowhere to call my own. I can tell you exactly when my life changed. It was 2nd September 1962. I would never forget it, as it is the day after my actual birthday. To most, their birthday is a special day that is celebrated. Looked forward to, as it is the one time that you are guaranteed to be the centre of attention. You get to feel special and wanted. Although for me, up until the day after my 7th birthday, I had never felt any of those things. I was there simply to be put up with. To be processed. People performed motions, actions of caring, but no actual care was taken of me. Well, not until a lady in her mid-30's, and a man who was at least 15 years her senior came to the home. They arrived in their highly polished blue Austin A30, and they took me back to their Farmhouse.

Mother and Father, they didn't feel the need to change my Christian name. After all, I was used to it, it had been my only constant. My surname was only changed to theirs due to the formal adoption process, and as that too began with a J, I continued to be known as CJ.

My name was the only thing that I kept from my past. After that date, my life was transformed. I was saved.

Post seven years, I had a wonderful childhood. My mother cooked the most fantastic of feasts. She was a natural homemaker. Fresh home-made bread, always plentiful. Jams and chutneys made from the hedgerows and the apple tree, that we had at the bottom of the garden. I liked nothing more than coming home from school, and to be greeted by her at the kitchen door. She would always ask if I was hungry? Of course, I was. I always was. What growing boy isn't? And in all truth, I still had the hangover from the Boys Home, of whether I would get fed, or whether one of the older boys would take my share. Anyway, she'd rustle up a doorstep sandwich, thickly spread with butter, cheese, ham, and chutney. I'd tuck in as if it was my last supper. But it never was. There were always more meals, more snacks being prepared. I'd only need to wait a further two hours, then Father would appear after a long day at the office. We would then be eating a leg of lamb with new potatoes, or cottage pie with spring greens. I had fallen on my feet, and although by the time pudding was on the table, and I was already full. I would still manage some of the homemade rice pudding, with a dollop of strawberry jam on the top.

Mother and Father were my world. I would do anything, and did do anything for them. This included years later, giving up my own life for them.

They had once rescued me, and I was indebted to do the same.

Scene Examiner Jones

It had been a pig of a week. I'd hardly seen John or the girls. I'd spent most of it in the lab; both days and nights, trying to see if I could give anything meaningful to Jo. The body when it was discovered, it was in such a state of degradation, and there was very little evidence that was of use at the scene. The killer was definitely forensically aware, and that is exactly what the criminal profiler that Jo had got on-board, had said in his report.

He was a funny little man, not the victim, I mean the profiler. He had an eclectic approach to dressing – He wore a green tweed suit and waistcoat, a yellow bow tie against a pale green shirt, as well as very highly polished tan shoes. He also wore bright red and yellow socks, which peaked out at the bottom of his trousers, and I mean one foot had a red sock on, and the other yellow! I only saw him briefly as he came to the lab. He wanted to talk more to my team, than he did to me. He told me squarely, that my DNA specialism wasn't really of assistance to him. He needed to know more about the techniques that the killer had used. He was strange, and very blunt in his delivery, and I felt that he could look right into my soul and it chilled me. It was as if he knew me better in an instant, than I knew myself.

It was decided amongst us "experts" in the Forensic Team, that the victim was not in the wood for more than 6 months, which put his death in and around the previous April. His bone density suggested that he was an elderly male. Although, even that was a little difficult to be completely accurate with, as they were severely damaged due to the heat of the fire. We got an estimate on height and body size, because some of the scorching from the fire had remained, providing an outline. But again, many of our conclusions were based on assumptions. And although it couldn't be proven, we believed that due to an indentation in one of the rib bones, the victim may have been stabbed, but without more evidence, or a weapon to compare with, it was just a working theory amongst the team.

Our killer was definitely forensically aware. They had torched him ensuring that any trace of usable DNA was destroyed. They had even been wise enough to remove the teeth and snip off the fingertips and toes, either that or they had been eaten by an animal and although possible, deemed rather unlikely. They could have saved some time in their disposal method by singularly using their bonfire technique, as the flesh would have melted within minutes, leaving behind no finger or toe marks. It was clear that they had used an accelerant. The fire would have been extremely hot to cause that amount of degradation. Mind you, as the old saying goes, 'if a job is worth doing, it's worth doing properly'. I admired them in a way.

I'd not had full sight of the 'Killer Profile Report', that Mr Bow-Tie had provided. (I can't remember his actual name. All this stress and lack of sleep has been getting to me), but I was aware that he believed them to be athletic, organised, and used to following instruction. When discussing his theories with one of the lab assistants, he'd said that they would have had to be 'disciplined'. He thought the killer knew the victim, and that this was possibly some sort of act of revenge. Personally, I could not see how he could ascertain any sort of profile. We had nothing, and even Mr Bow-Tie's report, was based wholly on assumption.   No actual facts.

I think Jo may try to see if the skull can be mapped, to get a facial ID, but with the damage, both from the teeth extraction and the fire, I think she'll be lucky to get anything.

DCI Jo Gordon

I got a promotion on the back of the rape conviction that Shirlie helped me secure, and I was moved to MIT. (Major Investigations Team).

I remember when I first discussed getting Shirlie with us full time, it was like trying to sell ice to an Eskimo. She just wasn't interested. She was pleased with the fact that she had "finally made a difference", as she put it, and I could see how getting justice for that victim had really impacted on her. However, she just wasn't interested in taking the plunge.

At first, I thought it was because she was determined on making the next big DNA discovery, and she had wanted her name in the history books; recognised for her pioneering DNA research. But on probing her, it wasn't that at all, she was scared. They talk about being in the police, and being institutionalised but it can happen to any of us, no matter where we work. We get so used to our surroundings, that we become fearful if we even consider changing them. It is no wonder that some of those old dears, have spent a lifetime, scanning cans of baked beans on the till at Tesco!

Of course, John didn't really help either. I had no idea that they were a couple. When I first approached her for help, she never mentioned it, but I suppose why would she? I'd bumped into him in the corridor at HQ. He was up there for a briefing, as was I, but for a different job. He said that he didn't realise that Shirlie and I were old school friends, and that she had mentioned the job offer to him. He tried to warn me off, saying that she was nothing like me, and that I should stick to recruiting from within. I took this to be a challenge. I never told Shirlie that her 'Hubbie' had tried to sabotage her "promotion." Well, it was a promotion in my mind anyway. The basic salary was almost double of what she was earning at the university, and I'd said that in her "downtime" if she wanted to continue her research, the Force would fully support it. Especially, if it led to me cracking the next big case, and me securing my next big promotion!

She did waiver a while, but after several coffee dates, and a bottle or two of Pinot at the local wine bar, she was much more receptive. Her main concern was that the job title of the role on offer was "Head of Forensics". I remember her words exactly, with a glass of wine in her hand…. "But I know nothing of the bigger picture. I am just highly skilled in one element, and even that I think, has been more luck than judgement. I have been lucky."

I asked her if she knew about budgets? If she could follow protocol? If she could make a reasoned argument for, or against a process? She rolled her eyes, partly because she was drunk, and partly because she thought my questions were a little ridiculous, replying…

"Well, of course, I obviously know about that! How else could I successfully manage my own research?"

"Well, there you go then…." I replied, "You can do the job!"

Upper Management were pleased with our new addition. They would never admit it, but it's still the same old boys club really, and they are always very receptive to someone who will advance their careers, as well as being easy on the eye; of which Shirlie was both. Well done me!

She started with us initially on a part-time basis, mainly because she wanted to finish off the research that she had committed to, and also as it was partway through the academic year, and she still had her teaching commitments to honour. She eventually joined us on a full-time basis in the late summer. I came to realise that she hated leaving loose ends.

Her joining was a big success. She's got attention to detail. She is meticulous. She thinks outside of the box, and although sometimes, she has to be reminded about the chain of evidence (as this is a new concept for her), all in all, she has been an absolute superstar.

I am only aware of one slight error, that she had made with the National Database. Apparently, she loaded her own DNA for elimination purposes but ran it inadvertently, by ticking the wrong box on our rather antiquated database. Thankfully, nothing came of it, and she's now been given a crash course on the system. Mind you, I think she now delegates this process, quite right too, we're not paying her that salary, for her to do the donkey work!

She also dislikes being called "Head of Forensics", so I still call her Shirlie, if it's just us, or Scene Examiner Jones, "Jonesy" at her request. Whatever floats her

boat! Always so modest. I don't share this trait. Loud
and proud that's me!

Shelley

Mum was right to make me wait until I was older before I read my biological mother's diary. It was weird to think that this childish handwriting, and content was the work of my mum. She had a formulaic approach to recording her day. It would always start with the time that she woke, be that by her Talking Bugs Bunny Alarm Clock, "Wake Up Doc!" (Reading this made me smile), or by her father gently waking her up on a Sunday, with a cup of tea in her favourite mug. It seemed that my mother, like me, loved her sleep, and getting up was a chore, again just like me. It was so nice to have a connection.

She would then move on to what she ate for breakfast. In fact, she always recorded what she ate. She clearly liked her food, and her own mother seemed to be a traditional cook, from the meals that she described. I could make out her favourite dinner was Toad-in-the-

Hole. Mine too. I wondered if I'd inherited this preference from her?

Her own mother was recorded in her day-to-day description, but with not much feeling. She didn't appear to get any love from her. Which to my mind was strange, because my own mother (my adoptive mother, it felt alien calling her that), couldn't and wouldn't show me anything other than affection. She showered me in both hugs and kisses. She was always telling me that she loved me. Not just verbally either. For example, in my packed lunch for school, as soon as I could read, she'd leave me little notes. Actually, even before I'd reached that milestone, she'd draw me love hearts on a piece of kitchen-roll, that she'd popped in for me to wipe my hands on. Just to let me know that she was there. I also only had to mention something that I was interested in once to Mum, and she would have scoured the shops to purchase whatever it was. To an outsider, you would think I was spoilt, and I guess to some extent

I was and still am. But I love my mum and dad (I mustn't forget Dad) with all my heart, and they have made me who I am today.

My own mother, however, she didn't seem to have that relationship with hers. Her father appears in all her writing to be the supportive and loving one. He seemed to have the time to spend with her. It looked as if A LOT of that time was in the pub, and maybe that's why she left me where she did? It was clear that he never ignored her whilst he supped his pint. No, they chose the songs on the jukebox together. The Rolling Stones features quite heavily. I can just imagine them singing the words to 'Satisfaction' at the top of their voices. He sounded fun. They even played pool together. Her gloating that she beat him regularly. I wonder how true that was? I am rubbish at both snooker and pool. Something I've definitely not inherited.

I do remember this one time in my school biology class. The teacher was talking about genes and inherited traits. It was the first time that I had really considered how different I was to Mum and Dad. They both had olive skin. Mine was porcelain white. Mum had brown eyes, and my dad's were green. Mine were a bright blue. Even their hair was dark and mine blonde. It sounds silly, but that very night after school, I went home via the shops, and I purchased a bottle of brown hair dye. My mum actually cried when she saw the result. "Oh, my goodness Shelley, what have you done? Your beautiful hair!" I just looked directly at her and said, "I just wanted to look like you and Dad. I wanted to belong." She just wrapped her arms around me and said, "Oh, Shelley darling, of course, you belong."

I'm not sure that Mum really liked the colour change, but she accepted it. She always encouraged and supported me in everything that I did. Even if that included me dying my lovely blonde hair so that I was more like her. I think in the end she understood why, and she took it as a compliment.

Scene Examiner Jones

I wake up in a panic. I have been doing that a lot lately. This time, however, I can see blue flashing lights at the edge of the blackout-blinds, illuminating the edge of the window frame. Obviously, my quick movement has disturbed John, as he's stopped snoring and I can hear him scrabbling at the side of the bed, looking for his glasses. "What's the matter, Baby?" I point in the direction of the window. He must be able to make out what I'm gesturing towards, even though it is still dark, and I've not made a sound. "What? The lights?" I manage to say "Yes" in a very quiet voice. I was not intending to sound so mouse-like, but that's all I can get out.

He gets out of the bed, and he goes to pull the blind back slightly so that he can see. "Oh, it's an ambulance. Looks like opposite. I can't really make out what's happening. Do you want me to go and see?"

Feeling a lot less panicked, I say "No Hun, it's fine, I don't really know what happened. I just saw the lights and thought...well, I don't really know what I actually thought...."

Getting back into bed, John lays down next to me. "Put your head on my chest, come on snuggle in, let's see if we can get you back to sleep."
I do as he says, I am shattered.

"This job is really getting to you; I knew you should never have joined. I know you, Baby. You can't take the stress. Why don't you look at going back to the University? They would snap your hand off."

His words anger me slightly, but I don't let it show. He really does think that I'm a weak female who cannot cope. Of course, I'm stressed, I feel like everyone is looking at me. I start doing my breathing exercises to try and relax me back into sleep. John needs no such help, as I can already hear that he is back snoring. It takes me a little while, but soon I am too.

DCI Jo Gordon

Do you think their destiny is set from the minute of conception? Or is it the fact that they are named something a little different, that dictates their fate? I often consider this when dealing with the scrote bags that darken my door. Whether if he or she had not been called Jed or Jordyn, and had been named Samuel or Sophia, that they would have gone down a different route? Not the path of drug use, and the resulting career of shoplifting and the robbing of old dears, just to support their disgusting habit?

Anyway, today I am presented with Gerald. He was definitely born with a silver spoon in his mouth. He is my bow tie, and tweed suit wearing profiler. I really hope that he is good. As so far, all of my avenues have come up with nothing, and I really need a break. He was recommended to me. He's well regarded in the field and another one, just like Shirlie who has numerous letters after his name, and journal after journal that has published his work.

He starts off by telling me that he has written a very detailed synopsis of the killer. He also follows this up with a health-warning, stating that his mind is like a computer. The facts that have been fed to him are what he has based his assumptions on, and therefore I am to be mindful of the old adage, (of which I have never heard...) "Garbage in, garbage out!"

I thank him for his time in helping me with the case, and he advises that if I have any queries, to contact him. He also makes an observation of Shirlie. Although he calls her my DNA Expert. "Very interesting woman that one. She says one thing, but her body language says something quite different." I shake Gerald's hand at the front of the building, having escorted him out, and consider only very briefly, what he's just said. I would never have called Shirlie interesting; I'm bored just thinking about her. *Fun to have a wine with and take the piss out of, but interesting... No never!*

I waste no more time on his comments, and make my way back up to my office and my computer. "Right, let's have a look. What can you tell me?" I say this as I double-click on his report, and wait impatiently for it to load on our outdated systems.

Shelley

It took a little while, but after I had dyed my hair, I finally managed to get my makeup just right, so that it complimented it. It was a little difficult for school, as makeup was strictly forbidden, but I would use a brown eyebrow pencil to shade in my blonde hairs, making my eyebrows at least visible, in contrast to my very pale skin and now dark brown hair.

In fact, after the initial shock, a number of my friends complimented me on my new look.   Some, out of envy, because my mum was seen as cool, letting me dye my hair. Others pointed out how my dark hair made my blue eyes really stand out.

When I was sixteen, one of my mum's friends bought me a makeup-set including eyeshadow and mascara. At the time, I wasn't overly fussed about makeup (I was a very young 16-year-old), but some months later after I had changed my look, I came across it. I experimented with the gold eyeshadow and black mascara, and I liked it. So much so, that on non-school days I would make myself up. Dad wasn't too keen, but when he grumbled, Mum would shush him, saying....

"She's just growing up. She's doing no harm. You can't protect her forever."

Anyway, it was either a half-term or a weekend. I'm not sure exactly when, but I was reading my mum's diary. I'd left it a while as I'd been doing my mocks, and I had needed to concentrate on studying. I'd spotted it one afternoon, when I was in my bedroom, having moved some revision notes on my desk. I picked it up and I laid on my bed. I opened it up and rested it on my pillow, and I started to read. Suddenly, large black splodges started to appear on the scribbled pages, and after a brief moment of confusion.... (As I did not know where it was coming from), I realised that I was crying and the black splodges were my running mascara.

My mum's dad had just died suddenly, and she had recorded all of her feelings in the diary. I could tell that she was broken. From what I could gather, he'd had a fit, been rushed to hospital and that was it. Gone! Her mother had fallen apart and had forbidden her from saying goodbye at the hospital. Later on, I considered that this might have been done to protect her daughter, but being so young at the time, I doubt that my mother would have understood. I hardly did, and I was at least a few years older than she was at the time.

There were a few blank pages after he had died when she did not write, but then the entries began again, but this time, much of what she wrote were questions. Why did this have to happen? What was she to do now? I couldn't work out if she was asking herself, her dead dad, or even God, but it was painful reading it. In fact, one of the pages had been half ripped out. I wondered what the bottom half of the page had contained, and why it was necessary for her to remove it, but I'm sure that she had her reasons.

I turned over the page to see if she had written more, but after that, all there were was further entries of what seemed complete and utter gibberish. Strings of letters that meant nothing. Unable to continue, I wiped my tears away and put the diary back in its place. I knew that Mum would be in soon with a cuppa, and to check on me and my revision progress. It was only later on when I was idly thinking about nothing in particular that it popped into my head. I didn't know why, but my mother had of course, switched to writing her diary in code.

CJ

Once, I asked Mother why she and Father had picked me. She said that as soon as she laid eyes on me, she knew that I was her son. With a huge smile on her warm loving face, she'd made reference to the milky-bar kid, saying "Only the best was good enough." I was very much aware that when I was younger, I had had a strong resemblance to the boy on the TV. In as much as I had blue eyes, wore spectacles and had blond hair. Anyway, I'd later found out that it was a done deal and it had already been arranged before they had even met me. They were willing to take an older child, and I was that older child, that the home was desperate to place!

I consider it all to be akin to the adverts you see on the TV now; those poor older dogs at Battersea. They look so sad and forlorn, just waiting for someone to pick them, rather than the bouncy new puppy in the next cage. I was the poor older dog, and thankfully, Mother and Father picked me. In that vein, I remained a faithful and thankful hound, so when they called for me, I came running.

After high school I'd gone on to college, and it was noted that I had a real creative flair. Mother and Father were keen to support me in all of my endeavours, so when I said I wanted to study Art at University, they gave me both the financial support and emotional encouragement that I needed.

It was there in the University Refectory, that I first saw George. He was quite a few years my senior, and he was a Lecturer. He smiled at me and I smiled back, and from that moment on, I was smitten.

I'd never been interested in girls and nor they in me. I think maybe I gave off the wrong vibe, but with George it was different, and the fact that he was older, it meant that I felt instantly secure in his company. Of course, nothing is ever simple. It was never a case of happily-ever-after. We couldn't just be together. George was unfortunately for me, already married. He had a wife and family, and I became a willing participant in an illicit affair.

George had a fabulous little flat. It was located in the heart of the busy University Town and after a short courtship, I very discreetly moved in and it was wonderful. During the week, when he was at the University working, I'd see him. He stayed at the flat with me, and at weekends he'd go home to his wife and family. It was a compromise, but one I was willing to accept. I was in love. Everything about George was almost perfect. He had dark smouldering eyes, pepper pot hair, and a strong physique. I'd finally found my soulmate, and other than Mother and Father, he was the only other person who made me feel special.

Now, as ironic as it sounds, George was sincere and loyal. He took great care of me. Those early years were amazing. Champagne breakfasts in bed, red wine by the fire and yes, I know he had a wife, but it didn't matter. In fact, and at that time, if he had divorced his wife and abandoned his children, it would have almost certainly led to the end of his career, and certainly our relationship. So, I was most happy being his "bit of stuff." It just worked. He kept his promise to her "till death do us part," and we happily skated over the "forsaking all others" bit. As I say, George was almost perfect, bar the minor bit of infidelity. However, even that didn't really matter. He was always honest with me.

Josephine

I knew that I had done the right thing, but walking away from her made me incredibly sad. I'm not sure if it was pure exhaustion, or a motherly instinct that had begun to kick-in, but I was sobbing. It was totally uncontrollable. My shoulders were heaving, and I could feel my stomach twisting. I was broken.

I felt in my trouser pocket and I was grateful that I still had three pounds. I had taken it from the money tin that Dad had given to me. Most of the money had gone on the B&B that first night, and then the train up to the Inn, but luckily, I still had a little change left.

It was still the right thing to do. What life could I offer a baby? Mum was so angry at me, and what if she grew up to look like him?

I got back to the Train Station in no time at all. My pace had been quick, even though I could still painfully feel every step. Giving birth would have been exercise enough, but I had just been on a cross country hike. I had comfort though. This nightmare would soon be over.

Luckily, the Ticket Office was still open. I dried my eyes, (there was nothing I could do with my blotchy face.) I then asked the rather rotund and balding man behind the desk for a single. He didn't even make eye contact; he just grunted the price and I paid.

I pulled my jacket close as I walked back out into the evening air. I'd left her wrapped in my jumper and my coat being thin, it really didn't provide the warmth that I needed. Crossing the tracks by the underpass to get to Platform One, was cold and damp. It only took a few minutes, but I was pleased to see the station light at the top, as I climbed the steep concrete steps. I made it just as the train came in, so I got straight on and settled on a seat by the window.

The carriages were quiet, hardly anyone else was travelling that night. There were no other passengers in my carriage, except an elderly lady. She was eating sweets from a paper bag. Every time that she selected another bonbon, I heard it rustle. She looked over when I got on the train and she gave me a smile, and I in return tried my best to smile back.

It was pitch black outside. I could see lights from the nearby houses flash past, as the train rocketed its way back down south. I was sat in silence, and I contemplated how my life had changed so drastically over the past few years. How had this happened? We then began to slow, I looked up and unbelievably it was my stop. I'd been so engrossed in my thoughts, that I nearly missed it. Quickly, I gathered myself together and I got off the train.

I knew it was the right thing to do. I was at peace with my decision, and with Dad's financial help, (the money from my tin) I felt comforted. It was like he was with me on my final journey.

Walking out of the Station, I checked my pockets, and I made sure that I had nothing on me that could link me to home, or the baby. I found her little ID wristband that I'd managed to slip-off of her. It showed the time and date of her birth. They'd called her female infant of Brown. But that wasn't my name. It meant nothing. I saw a bin at the edge of the station boundary, I walked over and I put it in.

After almost a 10-minute walk, I was by the side of the motorway. It was dark, and the traffic which was moving at pace had their headlights on.

I stepped out. Immediately it went dark and I was in pain no more. It was finally over.

Shelley

I had to wait until I could devote all of my time to cracking the code. This year was very important to me. I was in the middle of my GCSE's, and I needed to get the grades, so that I could carry on with my plan of getting the school to agree to the A-Levels, that I had preliminary selected.

Maths was fine, I'd always been naturally gifted. I'm not entirely sure where it came from, as I'd left both Mum and Dad behind in year 7 with simultaneous equations. I remember it well, Dad grumbling to Mum in the kitchen, when I'd once asked for his help… "I just don't see the point, when do you use those in the real world?" …. Mum had shushed him; always trying to keep peace, that was just her way.

Mum never pushed, but she did want the best for me. So, she asked an old school friend of hers, (a Maths

Teacher) to give me extra tuition. After that, I excelled and I never asked Dad for help again, well not in Maths anyway!

I needed to get at least a B in Double Science, but I wanted double A. Mrs Yardley said, "a B, would do." However, making do was never me.

I wasn't sure what I eventually wanted to do with my life, but I found Biology and Genes fascinating. (The unique code that made us who we are.) I think deep down, I wanted to know who I really was, so I put all of my efforts into making that happen.

I was a model student; both focused and driven. "Every teacher's dream pupil," well, so Mrs Yardley would often say. Although, I didn't care much for what anyone else thought, all I cared about was making the grade.

CJ

I will never forget that terrible day. That day changed my destiny.

It was dark and miserable. The rain was lashing down, and I vividly remember receiving the call. It was early morning. George had already left for work and I was busy working on a commission. (Oh yes, I'd graduated with a First-Class Honours Degree, and I was a fully-fledged Batchelor of Arts. I loved having a BA at the end of my name, it felt good.) I had finally achieved something.

Anyway, the phone rang and it was one of Mother's Carers. Dad had taken a tumble on the way to the bathroom and he was on his way to hospital, and would I immediately come home?

Mother had been diagnosed with early-onset dementia when she was just 49, and Father had been caring for her ever since. Latterly, however, he'd needed a little extra help. In the mornings and evenings, the carers came to help get her up, and then again at night, to put her back to bed. Thankfully they were at the house when he had fallen.

It was noticeable that nursing Mother full-time had taken its toll on Father. He was, after all 15 years older than her. I expect he thought all those years ago, when he had whisked her off her feet, that she'd be the one doing the caring in his later years, and not the other way around.

Anyway, I stopped what I was doing, and straight away I left for home. I was torn as to whether I should go to the hospital, or to the Farmhouse. Although, I didn't have to consider this for long however, as the choice was already made. The carer said she couldn't stay with Mother. She had other patients to get to. She had arranged cover until I got there, but then she'd have to leave.

The whole situation was tragic. Father didn't make it to the hospital. He sadly had a cardiac arrest in the ambulance on route, and died.

That was it. My life changed. I left the flat. I said goodbye to George and our wonderful life, and I moved back home.

John

My goodness, I'm looking over at her, and all I can see is an athlete. My wife is ripped. I can see her reflection in the bedroom mirror as she's getting dressed. I knew the counsellor said exercise would help, but this is a side-effect that I'd never expected! She is fit!

I come up behind her and I go to cuddle her, but she immediately pulls away.

"Please don't...." she says.
"What's the matter, can't I find my wife attractive?"
"Yes... sorry, but I've got a lot on my mind, I just can't at the moment."

Pulling back and feeling a little hurt, I go off to the bathroom to finish getting ready myself. I'm angry, and think to myself; I *know it's that bloody job, I knew she should have stayed where she was. It's done nothing but unsettle her. Why the hell did Jo have to convince her?*

The meddling bitch! Why didn't she just leave us alone?

CJ

After Father had passed, I became Mother's full-time carer. It seemed the right thing to do.

I tried keeping my and George's relationship alive, but it just became too difficult. He was getting older, and I wasn't so accessible. It hurt because I still love him with all of my heart, but it was never going to be the fairy-tale that I had dreamed of. All of us living together in the Farmhouse. No, that was never going to be.

These days, he'd only do ad-hoc lectures, so he was rarely at the flat, and a trip down to visit me, just seemed too difficult. I did try and get respite care for Mother, so that I could visit him, but it didn't work out. Mother got so distressed without a constant familiar face, (me or Father) and as Father was no longer around, that left just me.

Caring for Mother was hard. She'd have good days where we'd have really in-depth conversations; discussing politics (from the past), holidays, etc., and then, really bad days, when she didn't know who I was, or even really who she was. She'd regress to when she was a child. She was no longer a wife or a mother.

This one time, on one of her good days, she'd mentioned that she thought that I had a sister. She didn't know anything more, or couldn't remember, but it was strange to think that out there, I had a family.

DCI Jo Gordon

I had all the reports that I needed. My team had been working both day and night. Door to door enquiries, press appeals, POLSA searches. You name it, I chucked it at this investigation, and each and every time I came up empty-handed, it was so damn frustrating!

Due to the 6 months that had elapsed from the suspected date of kill, to the body's discovery, we had lost all of our usual avenues. There was no hope of CCTV and all the traffic cams had a rewrite of 28 days, so no hope of spotting a vehicle in the area via the ANPR either.

Gerald had highlighted the killer's meticulous planning in his report, and he said that almost certainly they would have needed a vehicle.

Forensics had discovered fibre remnants of a tarpaulin, so clearly, they had wrapped the body prior to torching it. It was unclear if they had moved the body, and the kill site was somewhere else, but as there was no clear evidence proving this one way or the other, we had no way of knowing if we needed to extend the scene.

We knew that the suspect had to be fit and strong. The victim's bone density, although it had suggested that they were elderly, the gravesite had also indicated that they were at least 6 feet tall. Moving a dead-weight of that height, would have required strength. We definitely had it that our victim was male and aged approximately 60 – 70 years old. But I still had so many unanswered questions...

Was the killer acting alone?

Were they male? A female?

I just didn't know.

Gerald thought it could be revenge, or passion because the bone damage suggested that the killer had used a knife. This too, however, was a curve-ball as this is typical for a spontaneous crime, and not one with such planning. And the killer certainly planned this. On reviewing the little evidence that we had, I suggested that nothing had been left to chance.

No teeth, no toes, no fingertips. I wonder if they'd removed the ears too? We've used the imprints from the ears before, in solving burglaries…. We'll not know for sure though, as they would definitely have melted in the heat of the fire, that's if they had even been left intact. I've seen burn victims before; the skin just melts. It's like butter. "Mmm Butter!" My mind wanders off-piste, as I realise that I'm hungry and I begin to route around in my tote bag for my "emergency flapjack". I always carry one, as I really do suffer from getting 'Hangry!' And it is not what I want when I'm trying to spot something, anything in the reports that could uncover a mistake made by the killer, or a clue as to my victim's ID. I definitely needed a clear calm head, and a full tummy!

After eating the very last crumb of my 'M&S All Buttery Flapjack', and washing it down with my now cold, takeaway latte. I study the forensic report again. It identified that petroleum was the accelerant that had been used. It also detailed the percentage of carbon, nitrogen, hydrogen, and oxygen that it contained, which had meant absolutely nothing to me, although I was assured when I'd previously asked one of the guys, that it was the type that BP or Esso sold. So, nothing special or uniquely identifiable there. *The DCI taps her pencil on the desk whilst thinking.... as she tries to find something, anything that can help...*

It fathoms me, how the neighbouring properties failed to spot a big bonfire in April in the wood? The smoke alone must have raised suspicion surely? I checked back on the CAD reports, to see if anyone had called it in. Nothing! It wasn't bloody bonfire night; it was April for goodness' sake!

I go through my profile again and I start bullet pointing the key points:

- *Meticulous*
- *Planner*
- *Athletic / Strong*
- *Rage?*
- *Revenge?*
- *Passion?*
- *Forensically aware*, I underline this.
- *Access to vehicle.*
- *Tarpaulin? Make? Readily available?*

I then remember that I'd asked for a facial reconstruction. Of course, let's chase that up. I send an email, marking it as urgent.

I then pop my head into the Main Office. It's full of my "Little Worker Bees". Yes, I am the "Queen!" I approach a female DC (I can't remember her name) blonde hair, slight frame and non-descript facial features. I get her to find out if we can chase up any info on the tarpaulin. She replies with a big grin, and she practically sings her response at me, "Yes Ma'am!" …. Ah bless her, so young, so eager to please.

She scurries off to action my request, and I go back to my office to re-read the report and see if there is anything that I have missed. I then head out to grab something for lunch at the Deli. The flapjack just didn't cut it…. I'm bloody starving.

CJ

At the time of Mother telling me about my sibling, I had tried to find her. I contacted Social Services providing my own birth certificate and adoption papers, but there was nothing.

Apparently, in the mid 1970's they had had a flood where a lot of their records were stored, and they think that mine, along with several thousand others, had had their history erased - just like that! There were no computers in those days with backup copies. Just paper records written in fountain pen, or typed. All now smudged by the water and totally illegible.

Mother was getting progressively worse, so I didn't have the time nor inclination to look any further, so I parked it to be revisited if I ever felt the need later on. It wasn't for another 20 years that I then began to wonder.

I'd nursed Mother till the end. She had sadly missed out on a telegram from the Queen by just 18 months. Not that she would have known what it was. Still, it was a shame. I would have enjoyed a little pomp, ceremony, and celebration. Not much really happened at the Farmhouse.

My life had been put on hold. It was time for me to do something for myself. It was time for me to find my sister.

DCI Jo Gordon

The tarpaulin was a dead end. Mass-produced, sold everywhere, and there was no means to track its origin.

After my chase up email, I had received an image of sorts. They said that it had been a difficult job, due to the damage to the jaw where the teeth were removed, and also the fire had not been kind. It made their reconstruction rather challenging. However, it was all I had and with some computer wizardry, I had myself a face.

They advised that they had opted for a balding appearance, as they thought a male aged 60-70 would almost certainly be losing his hair.

Anyway, I put it out to the press and to Crimewatch, and I grovelled yet again to Monroe for more budget to man the phone lines. Good job really, as we had an amazing response to the appeal!

Shelley

My goodness, my mum was clever. I didn't start trying to work out her cipher, until I was 18 or 19 years old. I'd been too busy trying to get the grades that I had wanted for university. I had decided to study Molecular Biology.

I chose Biology, Chemistry, and Maths, and as you can imagine it took up most of my time working towards the three A's that I wanted.

When I describe her as clever, I don't mean that she had a separate key for unlocking the code; not like Silvestri and his use of the Bible. Nothing nearly as sophisticated, but as a 13 or 14-year-old, grieving for her father, and when her entire world had been turned upside down, she was definitely advanced beyond her years. She used an uncomplicated and effective way of recording and hiding her innermost thoughts. She simply moved her alphabet along five spaces, so an A was now an F and that was that... I'd cracked it!

Once I had the code, I was off! I found it a fascinating insight into my mum's life. I would spend hours taking Mum's diary entries and decoding them.

I felt for Mum because it seemed she was really trying to please her own Mother. I wasn't sure if it was because she was missing the loving relationship that she had clearly had with her dad, or she just didn't want to rock the boat, and cause any more heartache for either of them.

Anyway, after the page that was half ripped out, my mum, as she had always done, she listed what she did that day. What she'd eaten, what she'd worn, even what time she was to go to bed. It wasn't inspiring. Not even that interesting, but it did give me an idea of where I'd come from.

From Mum's entries, it had become clear that she had embraced the Church. I suppose that she had no choice, seeing as her dad was no longer able to take her to the park or pub. And to be honest, she was probably a little too old for the former, and slightly too young for the latter, although not that it seemed to matter when she had been in her dad's company.

Anyway, there were countless entries of her going to Church. She'd sing in the choir. Help clean the brass, make tea and coffee for the meetings, of which there seemed to be many. WI, Sewing Club, Scripture Study. My mum seemed to help her own mum with all of them. The only thing that was slightly near her own age and where it seemed that she had friends, was the Church Youth Club.

The Youth Club seemed to be an extension of the Sunday School. Most of its young members were also in the choir (a good earner on a Saturday, when they would be paid to warble at the numerous weddings). The Youth Club did a lot of outside activities including utilising the large woodland area at the rear of the church.

Mum wrote a lot about a boy called Barnaby. From what I could gather, he was a little older than her, but not by much and she liked him as he was kind, and he would often draw her Garfield (the cat) pictures. He'd pen these funny illustrations whilst they were "listening" to sermon after sermon, and waiting for their cue to sing again. My mum appeared to be settled.

CJ

It couldn't have been any easier. I knew that Social Services were a dead-end in my quest in finding my sister, so I popped to the local library to find out how I would go about searching for an unknown family member.

It must have been fate because as I walked into the little village library, I bumped straight into a library helper. It had been raining and I was trying to shake off the raindrops from my umbrella, so I was temporarily distracted on my route in, hence the collision.

Anyway, she asked if she could help me and I said "yes!" Once I had explained what I wanted help with, rather than take me to the book section, as I had anticipated, she took me along to the IT Suite. "Suite" really was a gross exaggeration. It was a lone desktop with a sign hanging above it! That said, it was perfectly suited for my needs.

Anyway, Janice, who I later found out was just a volunteer herself. She helped me to google on the computer. This was something that I had never done before. She then helped me register with this ancestry company. She even created an email address for me. Something else, I'd never needed, nor wanted. But it did allow me to request a DNA sampling test. I opted that thereafter, that all other communication should be by way of the Royal Mail, as I wasn't really ready to embrace the digital age, even with Janice's help. For heaven's sake, I'd only just got a mobile, and to be honest, even with that, I kept forgetting to charge it or even take it with me!

I'd missed out on so much whilst looking after Mother, but I never regretted it. It was simply my recompense.

DCI Jo Gordon

I was gutted, this was not what I wanted on my blemish-free record. I solved cases; that was who I was, who I am, but this Bramley Wood case, it was my Achilles heel.

The facial reconstruction had thrown up hundreds of names, and my team had painstakingly followed up on each and every lead. Unfortunately, each and every person who we thought could have been the deceased, was very much alive and kicking. Now, don't get me wrong, normally that is a very good thing. The role of a Police Officer is fundamentally to save life and limb, but it's no-good thing when you are trying to identify a body of an individual, who has been murdered, cremated, and disposed of in the wood!

Monroe was less than happy with me. I had burnt up most of this year's budget, and he was getting pressure from the top. What could I do? I just didn't have anything, and Shirlie, well quite frankly, she had delivered me nothing.

I'm starting to think that I made a mistake by getting her on-board. I can see that neither her heart, nor head is in it. Either that, or she's got trouble at home. Maybe she and John aren't getting along. I don't really see how they fit anyway. Well, I suppose opposites are meant to attract, but I just don't buy it….

Anyway, mentally she's somewhere else at the moment. It's lucky that all she's really needed to do at present, is manage the budget and sign off on a few lab forms; because if I needed her actual expertise, I think I'd be hard pushed to get it.

Scene Examiner Jones

I'm tired.

I'm tired of all of this. Juggling the girls, John, my mum, as well as work; it has all become too much.

I feel much like I did after Maggie. I need some space. I've upped my exercise, but even that feels just like another chore. Another thing that I have to get done.

Don't get me wrong, going to the sessions do help, and as recommended, I have increased those too…. but I can't handle this anymore.

What have I done?

John

I'm worried about her. She's not coping and I don't
know why. I try my best to take the pressure off her,
but I can't always be there. It's the nature of what I do.
It's who I am.

She's also now got it in her head, that she no longer
feels safe here anymore. She thinks someone is
watching her. I've told her that she's just being daft. I
think this all stems from that case, and not being able to
give Jo what she wants! That bloody woman! All the
pressure that she has lumped on her... it's just not
right... And we've had a few isolated incidents locally.
That stabbing by the school, the hit and run, and now
the rape of that young girl up near the wood. It's done
nothing but unsettle her.

Once a friend described this area as a pearl in a cowpat;
sadly, not anymore, the pearl is engulfed! I know that

there is little we can do… all towns are the same these days. But I do wish I could get her to think more rationally, rather than her latest whim of wanting to pack it all in, and run away.

CJ

I'm so excited. It didn't take long for the kit to arrive. I had recognised the company logo immediately. I don't get much post up here as it's just me. It was unusual to hear the Postman's van wheels churning up the gravel at the front. Therefore, I was already at the door when he came to post it through the letterbox.

I was stood in the open doorway. "Here you go!" He said with a smile. I was like an excited child. It was just like Christmas.

Thanking him, I took the small package in, and I opened it at the kitchen table. I had to go and get my reading glasses, so that I could read the fine print instructions. I wanted to get this right. I wanted to make every effort in finding my sister.

My sister! The thought of not being alone anymore, it filled my heart with joy....

I meticulously followed what I had to do, providing a sample of saliva and sealing it up. Ticking that I wanted to be notified by post if there was a match. Putting on my coat, I then picked up the sample in the postage-paid envelope, and I made my way back into the village to send it off. Excitement fizzed throughout my body as I eagerly popped it in the red post-box on the corner.

The deed was done. No going back now. I just hoped that she was trying to find me too.

Shelley

Learning about Mum was fun, I could tell that she had a blossoming romance with this Barnaby, nothing physical just yet, if at all, but I could gather from her writing that she liked him, and from what she wrote of their interactions, he liked her too. It was sweet, he'd do her drawings and she'd take him slices of the many cakes, that she had baked with her mother.

My mum also mentioned another boy, or man called CJ. It seemed that he'd had a long-standing connection with the Church. It sounded as if he'd grown up at the Boy's Home that the Diocese supported. Mum mentioned in one of her entries that it had been CJ's birthday on 1st September. He'd been called up to the altar by the Priest, and everyone had wished him a Happy Birthday. It appeared to be a thing at St Mary's. You were presented with a religious book and also sung to. It was really rather nice.

As I continued to leaf through the diary, an old polaroid dropped out of the back cover. And in the same handwriting as the rest of the pages, and scribbled below the photo, it said Barnaby and CJ. It wasn't the best quality of photos, but you could just about make out their features. It was taken in a heavily wooded area. I wondered if it was taken behind the Church, that Mum was increasingly attending. I studied it briefly, and then I tucked it back in the pages of the diary. I was a little disappointed that it wasn't a picture of my mum. I longed to know more about her. I longed to know what she looked like. Was I like her?

DCI Jo Gordon

I knew what it was about, before I even made it to his office. I had been summoned.

I knocked gingerly. I could hear a muffled conversation behind the heavy brown door. It suddenly swung open and Monroe silently ushered me in, waving his arms, as he finished off a call on his mobile, and indicating to me that I sit down.

Monroe was better about it than I thought he would be, but the long and short of it, was that he was closing the investigation. It had drained his budget, and we were no further on, than we were on the day when we had initially found the body. I could tell that he was disappointed in me. Hell, I was disappointed in myself. I just couldn't get a break. Anyway, we had a trafficking ring that he wanted my team to concentrate on. His exact words were "Let's focus on the living, rather than the dead".

He said that the Body in the Wood case would go to the Cold Case Team, and it was now their responsibility to progress it; but I knew what he was saying. In reality the case was closed.

I was gutted. I had never once in my career not cracked a case. I heard what he said, but in all truth, it would never be closed to me.

Scene Examiner Jones

I took the call; I saw her name flash up on the display. So did John…. He gestured for me not to answer, but it was too late, I'd already swiped, and then I heard her officious voice on the other end of the phone….

"Sorry for calling so late!"

Ha! Sorry! She's not sorry…. She's got no sense of what's socially acceptable, and calling at 23:30 hours wasn't late for her. She's still working, so everyone else should be too!

"…. No, it's fine." I reply whilst stifling a yawn "What can I do for you?"
"Nothing really. I just wanted to let you know that Monroe has closed the case. He's taken me, and the team off it. Passed it over to Cold Cases."

"Oh right, thanks for letting me know. You OK with that?"

"No, not really, I'm disappointed, but what can I do? I have nothing…. You found me nothing!"

"Hey that's not fair, I can only work with what I have."

"Yes, I know, sorry Shirlie.   It's just it's the first case that I've not had a result with… I'm not used to it! Anyway, look, I've got to go!" And with that, she's terminated the call.

"What was all that about?" John asks me as I put my mobile back on the arm of the sofa.

"I'm not sure really…. I think she just wanted me to know that Monroe has closed the case."

"I'm surprised it took him this long to be honest, he's all about budgets these days…."

"Well, yes…" I reply, not wanting to get into a debate about work as it's late….

"Anyway, shall we go to bed?" I say, stifling yet another yawn.

When John gets into bed next to me, I was already snuggled down, and I went to give him a kiss goodnight. I was more than ready for sleep, but then his kiss lingered a little longer than the usual peck goodnight, and that was it. We made love. I don't know why, but I finally felt like I had a clear head, and I really wanted him. It felt amazing!

Shelley

I stuffed my translations to the very bottom of my bedroom bin, and with tears streaming from my eyes, I pulled on my trainers and I ran straight down the stairs. I opened the front door and I was away, and out of the house.

It's not true, it can't be? I'd been reading Mum's diary again, and I had come to believe by the way she'd written about Barnaby, that I was a product of young love and naivety.

Up until my conception, my mum was full of hope. She had endured the pain of losing her father, and the lack of affection from her own mother. She'd found comfort in the Church. Comfort in her friend and her potential boyfriend Barnaby. He was a little older, but nothing criminal and he was fun, often teasing her. I could tell in her writing, it was upbeat. Well, it was up until that day.

The Youth Club were camping overnight in the wood at the rear of the Church. My mum practically had to beg her mother to let her go. I think her mother was concerned over her safety in the woods overnight. My mum had assured her that some of the older members of the Youth Club, were also camping, including CJ. The very fact that he would be there, it had swung it for her. Her mother had a real admiration for CJ. Apparently, he'd not had the greatest of starts in life, but through the love of Christ, he'd succeeded.

According to her mother, he was taken into care as a wee lad and through no fault of his own, the numerous adoptions just didn't work out. So, in the face of adversity, he had brought himself up. And to his credit, rather than become a waster, he'd got himself an apprenticeship. He was doing well as a Mechanical

Engineer. He really was the blue-eyed boy. He could do no wrong. Her mum saw him as a saint with a spanner!

However, on THAT night he'd followed my mum to the rear of the Church. She'd gone looking for Barnaby, who had gone to source some matches for the fire...

My mum wasn't sure, but she thought CJ was drunk. He seemed funny, and his breath smelt like her father's used to after he'd been to the pub. My mum described his behaviour as "acting weird", noting that CJ had cornered her against the stone wall at the rear of the Church. He complimented her figure and her striking blue eyes. Describing them as gem-like. She described how he had leaned in for a kiss, and that she had instinctively turned away.

Reading on I could tell that she was horrified. However, undeterred, he coerced her. He then started quoting the bible at her. "Romans 16:16 greet each other with a holy kiss."

I'm not sure what happened next, my mum didn't graphically document it, but I knew that she had been raped....

I knew, there and then, that I wasn't created in an act of love. No, I had been created during an act of violence. It was there in black and white. My mother's perceived protector was nothing more than a wolf in sheep's clothing. He was a rapist and I was the unfortunate result.

The realisation of my origins crushed me, and I didn't know what to do or how to feel. It was no wonder that she abandoned me.

John

She's still not giving up on moving. She's forwarded me so many houses that I am supposed to "consider" …. and the schools; goodness me! She just won't stop! It's Ofsted this, Ofsted that! She's already got Maggie and Heidi starting at their new school, and we've not even done one house viewing yet, or even got ours up for sale! I'm not even sure that I want to move. What is she running away from? I just wish she would talk to me. She is such a closed book; it's just not healthy.

Shelley

My mum finds me at the park. It's pitch-black and I'm sat on a swing. I don't have my coat with me, and it's raining. I'm wet through. In her hand, I can see that she has my now soggy translations.

With tears in her eyes, she asks me straight. "Shelley love, have you been raped?" I shake my head and mouth the words "No." I am sobbing, and tears are uncontrollably falling from my eyes. "Well, what is this darling? I found these in your bin, if it's not you, then who? You didn't even take your coat, and you always feel the cold... I didn't know that you were even out. Answer me darling... what is going on? I found these, and after I read them, well I just thought the worst." ...

She sat on the swing next to me, and straining to hold my hand. "Shelley, please love, what's the matter, who were you writing about?" I turn to her and say "It's

Mum's diary. She was raped. I'm here because she was raped…"

I've said it out loud, and it feels all the more real. My mother, she looks at me, her eyes glistening. I can see that she is anxiously searching for the right thing to say. She says nothing. Instead, she gets up off the swing and takes me up in her arms, all five-foot-five inches of me.

At that moment, my mum with a simple hug, she took away all the pain and sorrow that I felt. The pure revulsion of who I was. A rapist's daughter. My mum, I realised doesn't care about the past, she loved me no matter what. No matter where I came from, and for that I was grateful. All Mum ever cared about, was that I had a safe and secure future.

DCI Jo Gordon

The file had been passed to the Cold Case Team. I was no longer SIO (Senior Investigative Officer). I had my focus on this trafficking epidemic. It seemed to be the latest thing in the world of organised crime. Don't get me wrong, it's always happened, but of late either they are getting really sloppy, or we've been getting better at catching them.

Anyway, I was walking through the Front Office, to discuss some local resourcing with the Borough Commander and I overhear a female dog walker. She is trying to hand in a key that she had found in the wood. Uniform were covering the desk, and they were busy sending her on her way saying…. "We don't accept lost property anymore." And…. "Maybe try posting it on a local Facebook page to see if anyone has lost it."

She was just on her way out of the door when something made me ask her "Which wood?" She replies "Bramley, you know, near where you found that body!"

That was it, I had her lightning quick back in that Front Office and a local DC taking her statement. I had such a good feeling about it. I was fizzing!

Shelley

After that day when I had learned the truth of my beginnings, I went back to the diary to read more about what had happened. I had hoped that although my mum had been raped by that monster, that he still might not be my father. I remained optimistic that Barnaby could still be my dad. I'd hoped that my mum had sought comfort in him after what had happened, and I was the result.

It took me a while to decode the additional pages. My mind just wasn't in it, but no, it wasn't meant to be. There it was, in black and white. I was conceived that night. I read on further, and it transpired that initially, my mum didn't realise that she was actually pregnant. From what I could gather, she was a late developer and had only recently started her periods. She did not know her cycle; it was all new to her. So, a missed one or two did not set alarm bells ringing. It was only once her knickers had started to get tight, and her shape was changing that her own mother had started to get suspicious; that and the need to vomit every morning, finally confirmed it. She was pregnant.

It was so sad reading how my mum's life was falling apart. Her mother chastised her, calling her "Slut" and "Whore." She'd prayed daily that my mum would miscarry. Well, she couldn't take her for an abortion. She was, after all, a devout Catholic!

Anyway, the entries were pretty bleak. My mum had tried to tell her that she was raped, but her mother would have none of it. Preferring to believe the worst of her own daughter, over the truth about the saintly CJ.

My mum was hidden away. Her mother had invented some sort of illness to cover the fact that she was no longer seen in public. No church or school. I don't know how she got away with it. These days social services would have been all over them. I suppose being in the late 70's early 80's, things were a little different.

The last entry that she made must have been just before I was born. She had described how she was feeling and that her bump seemed to have dropped. She also detailed how her contractions had felt. From my own experience, (some years later) I would have said that the early pain that she documented, would have been Braxton Hicks, but as she made no more entries after this point, I could not know for sure.

I closed the diary and locked its pages back up. I had already added my translations to it. What else was I to do with them? I didn't want to put them in my bin and run the risk of my mum finding them again. After all, she'd already given me back the other damp pages, so I suppose it was a complete set.

Mum was right. I was a product of my own destiny. She said that to her and Dad, I was a gift. It didn't matter how I got here, all that mattered now was who I was, and who I was going to become. Mum said they'd rescued me as a baby, and they would protect me from harm, forevermore. Don't get me wrong, the truth had its impact. After I'd learned the history of my beginning, I undertook regular counselling. It was a necessary prerequisite to my future well-being. I needed it.

I also put my heart and soul into my studies. I excelled, not only obtaining a First-Class Honours Degree, but also a Masters to boot. It wasn't until some years later, and after I'd completed my Doctorate, and had an accomplished career, that I really began to consider where I had come from.

Gran and Pops had passed away within months of each other. They were my dad's parents and although obviously not blood relatives, they were the only grandparents that I had ever known. Gran was a natural homemaker, always baking, knitting and sewing. School holidays at their guest house by the sea, was the most magical place to stay…. Pops had been a pilot in the war and an engineer. Then, in his later years, he had studied to become a horologist, (a clockmaker).

Their guesthouse was always alive with ticks and chimes as the various timepieces made their presence known…. In fact, that was Pops through and through… He would always make an entrance. By way of his vibrant clothing; bold three-piece suits, teamed with a bow tie and polished shoes, and by his loud singing voice. He'd invariably belt out a 1940's hit as he entered the room. "Keep young and beautiful" was one of his staples. He was such an energetic character…So, when he collapsed at the care-home, and died only three months after Gran, there was a big hole left behind. It made me realise that Mum and Dad were my only elders left, and although I was not alone, I did feel at times as if I were…

I had no paperwork that could locate my birth mother, and the name "CJ" was pretty vague, in helping me to locate my rapist of a father. After much consideration, I decided to submit my DNA to an ancestry database. I was curious to see if I could locate any blood relatives. Well…. I got as far as signing up online and requesting a kit.

John

It's only a bloody key! You should hear her, it's like she's cracked the case! She is back to her badgering old self. Why can't she just leave her alone? I know she's the Head of Forensics, but for heaven's sake!! It's not her specialism, and we all know that moveable evidence is just that, it's moveable! There is little or no evidential credence. It's not like it was found at the same time as the body. The forensic and search teams meticulously combed that woodland floor, and they found absolutely nothing.... but a dog walker... months later finds a key, and she's back on her high horse demanding this and that. My god, I have absolutely no idea what I saw in her at Training School. She was the biggest mistake of my life. They say that opposites attract, but me and her? It makes me sick just thinking about it.

Anyway, after the excitement brought on by the idea of moving, and her obviously clear-head, due to the closure of the case, she is now back to not sleeping, and she tosses and turns for most of the night. I'm sure that she's even taken to grinding her teeth! She looked horrendous this morning. Even the girls noticed. Heidi had handed her Mummy, her favourite bear. It broke me as I heard her little voice say, "Here Mummy…. Teddy will make you better."

I'm not even sure that she heard her, as she just looked up from her coffee, and gave a very weak smile. She then continued just staring into the distance. It was a good job that I was there to distract Heidi. If I hadn't made the promise of pancakes with chocolate-spread, I really think that she'd have been hurt by her mother's non-plus reaction. I just don't know what to do with her.

Shelley

I don't even think I sent it off…. I um'ed and ah'ed that much. I knew what it was as soon as it came in the post. As no one was around so I did the test immediately… Well, not a test so much, but I provided my sample. I sealed it up and was getting ready to go straight out to post it, when nerves got the better of me. My heart started pounding, and my mouth went dry. What was I doing? Do I really want to open up Pandora's Box? It's not like my mum fought for me, and I was taken away from her against her will? No, she put me in a pub doorway. I mean what was she thinking? Did she want the local alcoholic to take me on? Why did she even consider that was the best place to leave me? Why not leave me at a hospital or a police station? Or a church for that matter? …. For heaven's sake, I know this all started there, but they are not all the same. This whole country was once built on the teachings of the bible. It had been the backbone of society, with all of its rights and wrongs.

I then started to consider HIM…. Yes, my rapist father. What would I do if I actually found him? How would that make me feel?

Anger welled up inside of me, and I chucked the sample on the kitchen counter, along with the rest of the mail. I'll sort it later *(I thought)* but right now, I need to go for a run. I needed the release before I burst into tears, or broke something. I had never felt anger quite like it!

CJ

I certainly wasn't expecting a response straight away. I was excited, however. I had hope.

My days were pretty uneventful after Mother had died. To pass the time, I did a couple of charity-shop runs with their clothing. I had not really had the inclination whilst Mother was still around. I was fearful of unsettling her further, by getting rid of Father's belongings. What if she'd opened a drawer and his socks and underpants were no longer present? Or she had noticed that his hat was no longer on the stand? No, it was easier back then to leave things as they were.

I just felt that now was the time, and to be honest, it gave me something to do. After all, I didn't have anything else to keep me occupied. I had been Mother's full-time carer for most of my adult life. Sadly, however, now that I was left without a care in the world, rather than feeling liberated, free almost, I felt more trapped than ever. I was scared. The world had moved on at a lightning pace, and I felt like I had no means of catching up.

For my own sanity, I kept my and mother's routines. Roast on a Sunday. Countdown in the afternoons, Horlicks before bed. I had tried to make contact with George, but the landline no longer connected, and my letters which I sent, all came back as addressee unknown. My guess was that he had fully retired, and he had left the world of academia behind. He no longer required our little nest. Or... my other thought which saddened me greatly, was that he had passed away. He was, even back then when we met, much older than I was. He would have aged just as I had.

I started painting again. I still had lots of my art stuff from when I moved back home. I just had to go to the local art shop to re-purchase my oils, as they had long since dried up. Painting, and keeping my old Vauxhall Astra spick and span kept me occupied. I had no need to work. I had saved a lot of the money that I had received as a carer, and Mother and Father had also left me a tidy sum. Additionally, I was not that far off retirement myself. Ironic really, as what would I be retiring from?

Anyway, two years had passed, and I had almost given up hope, as the only thing that the postman delivered were bills. Then one day, a letter arrived from the DNA people. I recognised it instantly, the logo was very distinct. Two strands entwined. I picked it up off the mat, along with my water bill and I went through to the kitchen. Having located my reading glasses, I opened the crisp white envelope. My heart was pounding.

It had all the usual pleasantries...

Dear Mr So-and-So;

Thank you for choosing us in your search. We are delighted to inform you that we have located a match….

I couldn't believe it!! A match! I finally had a family! I was no longer alone…

It provided me with the full name, address, and contact number and it advised of a 99.99% probability of parentage.

I was shocked…. Parentage!? How could this be?

I had never even kissed a woman, and certainly never been close enough to father a child!

There must have been some mistake? My hopes were immediately dashed. I had the full details of my supposed, what? …. Child?

They, like me, had apparently consented at the time of submitting their sample, to not going through an intermediary. Well, the thought of having to wait for a third party, would have drawn out the process, and I was so excited at the time of submitting my sample, that I didn't want to waste any time with a go-between. I was now thinking that a third party, would have been really useful, because I could have queried the result.

There was an 0800 number to call, but when I dialled, it wouldn't connect. So, feeling extremely disappointed, I threw the paperwork on the kitchen side. I was so disheartened.

It wasn't until later that day, that the house phone began to ring. This was unusual as it never normally did. I had no one to call me. Well, not unless you count those PPI calls. I've never had PPI, and I never needed any form of credit…. but sometimes, it's quite nice to have a chat with someone. So sometimes I play along. It's the same with the personal injury claim calls. Again, I play my part, well I do until I realise that they are taking me seriously, and then sadly I have to curtail the call. In fact, only last week I was speaking to a lovely lad... I think he said that he was from the Wirral; such a nice accent.

Anyway, this call was neither of these types... The caller was softly spoken. They advised me that they'd got my contact details from the DNA database, and that they believed that we were related. We chatted briefly, and I explained that I had indeed got a similar letter, and that I had been searching for my sister.

I gave a potted history, and I advised that I was adopted, and I had wanted to find any living family. The caller went silent very briefly, and then they told me that they weren't my sister, but her firstborn. They said that their mother had passed, but this letter had come to the house, and it had been opened out of curiosity. They could not provide an explanation for the parentage part, nor the fact that the dates of birth did not marry up, but I was assured that they had queried the bloodline, and the company had confirmed that we were indeed related.

My heart immediately felt lifted, I couldn't believe it. I was sat there in the farmhouse kitchen, and at the other end of the phone was my family. I had to meet them. I was no longer alone

The previous February before the body is discovered

Preparation is key. Fail to prepare, and be prepared to fail.

I couldn't believe it, I had him. I knew where he lived, I had chatted to him, and to an outsider, he had seemed like a kindly old gentleman, and not the rapist that he actually was.

I wasn't really sure of the plan. Did I even have one? I had never really thought any further on, than just speaking to him on the phone…. Thankfully he was so forthcoming, and it was quick thinking on my part, to explain that the sister that he was looking for, was in fact, my mother. I am so pleased that I was deliberately vague when I had initially made the call. He rather handily filled in all the pieces, and I made-up my own story to fit.

Anyway, I wasn't going to be fooled by him. I wanted answers, remorse, an apology, maybe? I wasn't sure what I was going to do, but I knew I needed a means of protection. I didn't want to report him, or go through any official channels. No, I didn't want that. It would cause too much pain. All of this out in the open for everyone to read and digest. Sharing our dirty washing…. The thought of it made me shudder…. No, I just wanted to give him a little taste of his own medicine, and to find out who he really was. Was I just going to hurt him, or something else?

I started thinking about this issue, and then I considered the worst-case scenario. Murder? Was that really my goal?

I did my research. I needed to be sure, that if it came to that, it didn't get traced back to me.

Over the months, in between casually chatting to CJ, (his nickname), I got organised. He initially requested that I called him 'Uncle CJ'. He said that he was a traditionalist, but I had said that it was too soon for that, as I had yet to build any sort of relationship with him. His voice sounded a little disappointed, but he said that he understood, and maybe I'd reconsider after we had met?

Anyway, I bought a knife, hammer, tarpaulin, ratchet straps and bolt cutters. I also got a canister which I filled with petrol. I couldn't take the risk of doing one big shop. My shopping list had murderer written all over it!!

No, I was cleverer than that. I split my purchases over several locations. You can't be too careful in this day and age. Big-brother is everywhere. I also only used cash, so not to leave any sort of paper trail…. I then stored them in the shed outside. No one other than me ever went in there. I was the gardener at my residence, and the shed was my domain.

What was I doing? I wondered this very briefly, and then I remembered. He was the enemy. He was a rapist.

DCI Jo Gordon

What is it with that bloody woman? I give her the evidence which she is supposed to process, or in this case, give to one of her lackeys, and she is only bloody talking about bleeding providence! I get that it is moveable. I get that it may not be involved in the case. I know all this, but it's all I have got, and I have a hunch. A gut feeling. I'm bloody good at my job, and I know that little rusty key, it holds the key to unlocking this whole case. (Ha-ha, no pun intended!)

Shirlie is just being awkward, the sooner that she and lover boy make the move that she keeps talking about, the better. Then I can finally get a Head of Forensics, who works my way, and things actually get done. She is like a walking SOP these days, quoting budgetary process and allocation of resources, and of course the chain of evidence. In a nutshell, she seems to have gone the way of Monroe, and she cares more about the sums and policy, than getting the actual job done!

It's so bloody frustrating!

John

We have finally found a house, and I actually really like it. My goodness, and so does she... She's not stopped talking about the place... The girls can have their own rooms, and there is enough space for us both to have an office, rather than being cramped, and working at the kitchen table. I see exactly now what she means. By just moving out a little, you get so much more. It's a no brainer!

The local schools seem wonderful, great reviews and we've even met a few of the parents. We have been invited to a few playdates already. It's such a village feel. You know, friendly and everyone looking out for each other... I can totally picture us there...

She has also decided to quit her job. She's had a word with HR at the University, and there is a teaching post that will be available in a few months. It's part-time and it will fit around the girls. Yes, she will need to commute, but it will definitely work.

This all seems too good to be true. I think I might just get my wife back. I am just so excited about the prospect.

CJ

So, we've only gone and done it! We've agreed to meet and I can't wait!

They wanted to meet up near an old church. I didn't ask why, but I am sure that they have their reasons. I've been to the shops and bought a new pair of trousers, a shirt, a tie, and a jumper. I know the weather is beginning to warm up, but it is April, and the evenings can still get chilly. I also want to look my best.

I have already looked at the map, and it's not that far, 30 miles max. Although, I do need to get a move on, as I really don't want to be late. I comb my hair in the hallway mirror. I am so lucky that I still have a full head of hair, even at my age. Father, bless his soul, he was bald as a coot!

I walk out to the front of the house, and I get into the car. I turn the key in the ignition and nothing! Not even a splutter. The car battery is dead. I start to panic. What can I do? I suppose I can rearrange, but how will that look? Taxi, I'll get a taxi! I call up the company that Mother and I used to use regularly. The Controller advises me that they cannot accommodate my request. It is at their busiest time of the afternoon. They will all be on the school run in an hour, and there is no time for them to drop me, and to get back in time for their regular pickups. I desperately try to think of other options.... Then it comes to me. Of course! Father's car! His old Austin A30. It's in the garage. It was like a museum piece, so well preserved. My father had doted on that car, almost as much as he had on Mother. I search for the garage keys, and the car keys too. Both are in the mess that is the kitchen drawer.

I go outside and open the door to the garage. I struggle a little as the wood has warped. I walk over to the car which has been sleeping for years. I then hurriedly take off the tarpaulin that covers its bodywork, and use the now rusty key to unlock the driver's door. I then anxiously put the key in the ignition, and by some act of God, it turns over! I can't believe it. I notice one of the rear tyres is flat, but nothing is going to stop me now. At pace, I go back to my car for the foot pump and bring it back to the garage…

I am sweating after the exertion of pumping up the tyre. I don't look quite as well presented, as my hair now is slightly curly due to this, but I am finally on my way. I'm pumped, just like that tyre. I'm finally going to meet my family.

I hear the wheels shift on the gravel as I turn into the lane from the driveway. I have not even considered the fact that I am not insured to drive this car, or whether it is even roadworthy. Practical thoughts couldn't be any further from my mind. At last, I'm off to meet my family

and I'm absolutely elated!

Scene Examiner Jones

A warm April afternoon, prior to the woodland discovery

"What do you mean you can't be in with the kids? John, you promised!"

"Yes, I know, but now I am unpromising. You know what my job is like. I'm on call.   I have taken the call, and now I need to go!" He says this quite gruffly, so I know that there is no changing his mind, even for the hour or so that I need.

We are all stood in the hallway; Me, Mum and John. I have my gym clothes on and I'm holding my sports bag. I was just about to go to a body-pump class. I really needed it. I have been so stressed with the new job. I don't really know what I am doing, but I know that if I am to get any sleep tonight, and be half a good Mummy, I need to go and work this stress out.

Mum is also in the hallway; she's got her suitcase. I'm dropping her off at the Station, for her to pick up their car. Dad left it there earlier when he caught the train into town. Mum was on her way home. She had stayed for the last two nights. She had looked after the girls, as both John and I have been on earlies. She's shattered, I can see it in her eyes. She also looks stressed, or like something is worrying her. Poor Mum, she never gives herself a break...

"John! Please! Can't you just delay it by an hour? That is all I need!"

"No darling, I can't. Why are you so desperate to go anyway? It's just a class!"

Through gritted teeth, I say "It's not just a class! You know what it means to me. Anyway, if I miss it again, they will fine me and I won't be allowed to pre-book anymore. I'll have to take my chances each week, and you know I can't be doing that!"

The doorbell rings, it's Jeanette from next door. I open the door.

"Oh, hi Jeanette, great to see you, it's been a while."

"Well yes, we've just got back from the Gite, much better April weather here, than there. I saw that both cars were up the drive, so I thought I'd pop in and say hello."

"Where are my beautiful girls? Goodness... I've missed them" …. And with that, both Maggie and Heidi appear, both eager to get to Jeanette first. Both desperate for a big bearhug.

"Oh sorry...you look like you are all going out? Have I come at the wrong time?"

"No Jeanette, don't worry, I was going to a class, but John's just been called in. And Mum, well she's shattered, so she's just off too. I'm not going anywhere!"

I say this whilst I glare at John. I am still angry that his job has a knack for messing up all of our, I mean MY plans…. Jeanette sensing an atmosphere, she looks away and then she begins coughing uncontrollably, albeit for only a very brief moment…. "Are you OK?"… I say this a little concerned.

"Oh yes… sorry about that. Don't you worry about me, something just caught the back of my throat. Petrol, oil, or something?"

"Oh, really? Well… I can't smell anything…." I look at John and Mum, but they don't appear to have noticed a smell, or if they have, they don't say so.

"Right then…" and clearing her throat again, Jeanette begins…. "How about I look after the girls? … What will you be? An hour, or two?"

"Oh my god! Really?" I say my words quickly, before she reconsiders…. "Are you sure that it's no bother?"

"None what so ever. I have missed them…." She clicks straight into babysitter mode and asks… "Have they eaten?"

It was 4 o'clock, they had only been home from school for half an hour. "No," I reply "but if they get hungry, there is pizza in the fridge…. Oh, Jeanette, you are an absolute lifesaver!"

Each of us kiss the girls before we all leave on-mass. John heaves his big kit-bag into his car boot and he's gone. I hear his wheels screech, as he turns off the drive. I then drag Mum's suitcase out of the house and pop it in my car boot, alongside my gym bag.

"Blimey Mum!" I say as I comment on her suitcase's weight… "What have you got in here? Rocks?" She just smiles, as if she's not heard what I have just said. She has already settled herself in the passenger seat and has strapped herself in. She leans over and grabs my hand. She then says "You know darling, it will all be alright". I smile back at her and think to myself... *Oh, Mum… I know it will!*

DCI Jo Gordon

It takes a while, but forensics finally take a look at the key. Shirlie gives the go-ahead, but it's under the proviso that it wouldn't hold up in court. The chance would be a fine thing. I don't even know who the victim is, let alone me getting a suspect to court! It turns out that it's the key for an old Austin. I would have thought that they would have been extinct by now... Surely the chassis would have eroded, just like the key; which is covered in a deep layer of orange rust, and to be honest, I can understand why it wasn't spotted by our search team.

I had put a bulletin out on the briefing, just to see if any of the Local Ward Officers, remembered seeing an old Austin in the area, close to the time of the murder. I had already reviewed the scene notes, and nothing had been recorded at the time of the body's discovery. Any vehicles that were, were all accounted for, but by fluke, one of the Safer Neighbourhood Officer's had noted an old A30. He went back through his pocketbook. One of the 'Neighbourhood-Watch Scheme's Old Dears' had reported it as abandoned a few months prior to the body's discovery.... *Ah... so they do notice something, after all!*

He provided the registration number, but unfortunately, it came up as a dead-end. Literally, I mean as the registered keeper was deceased, and there was no insurance currently held...

Apparently, the Council had removed it due to its 'poor state of repair.'   It had a flat tyre or something like that. It had been taken to one of the Local Car-Pounds, but PNC (The Police National Computer) didn't say where.... So, I have put in a request to the Council to try and find its location. It's just a waiting game now, to find out my answer...

Bramley Wood - A warm April evening

So, I made it! I really didn't count on being delayed, but luckily it looks like he isn't here yet. I parked up in a lay-by, not far from the Church and I took my contingency plan purchases into the dilapidated shed at the edge of the wood. I kept the knife and tucked it in my waistband. I felt strong, just like a gangster. I was prepared.

I didn't actually see him arrive…. I thought I would have heard his car, but no.   One minute I was alone, and the next, there was an elderly male, with a flop of golden hair in front of me. I instantly recognised him….

"Uncle CJ? Is that you?" He turned to face me.
"Yes, yes…. Oh, it's so wonderful to see you."
He came straight over and he hugged me tight. My body instantly stiffened….
"I'm so pleased I made it. Car trouble…"

I nod my head, thinking to myself...So that's why I didn't hear you arrive?

"Right then..." he says. His voice is excitable, and his eyes are glistening....

"tell me about yourself. I want to know everything."

He isn't how I imagined he'd be. Maybe age has softened him. But I'm not going to be fooled however, or give him any leeway. I know exactly what he is. He is a rapist, and I want to hear his explanation.

I say to him.... "Shall we walk and talk?"

"Yes ok." He replies smiling at me....

We walk around the edge of the church ruins, and approach the flint-stone rear wall... I pause, close to where it happened.... I turn to face him, and I study what he is wearing. He is well turned out, in a shirt and tie with a matching jumper and coordinating trousers.

He has even polished his shoes. He has clearly made an effort…

"So then, is it good to be back?" I say questioning…. He looks over at me, puzzled…. Answering… "Back where?"
"Here of course…. The scene of your crime!"

My eyes fixed on his. I think to myself…. "Don't you dare, don't you dare deny it…." And do you know what?! He bloody well does! He casually replies to me…

"I don't know what you mean, I've never been here before." Then he goes on to say, "It is quite beautiful…. You really wouldn't know this was here, unless you're local. It's so overgrown, you would never see it from the road…."

I try to remain calm, but I can't believe how blatant he is. No flicker of remorse, nothing.

"You call this place beautiful? Is that what you really think?"

I can feel the anger bubbling up inside of me... He had described it as beautiful. And to an outsider, yes maybe, but not to me, I know this scene. This place hosted a horrific event all those years ago, and it was far from that! The arrogant, sick, bastard!

I look directly at him and questioning him, I say... "Do you really not remember this place?"
"No, why? .... Should I?"
"Well, what about her? Surely you remember what you did to her?"
"Well, no!" His voice is starting to quiver. My veil has clearly slipped, and the anger in me is showing.

"Right... you come with me. Let me show you something."

Hesitant, he follows me away from the stone wall of the Church and into the wood, and past the shed that's looking after my provisions.

"Right, here we are!" I say this, whilst looking about my surroundings, and he mimics my actions. I can see him also surveying the scene. I begin rooting around in my pocket, and then I pull out an old polaroid photo...
"Take a look, who do you see?"

He pulls out his glasses from his top shirt pocket, just beneath his cotton blue jumper. He puts them on. Squinting a little, as he studies the photo.

"Well, that's me." He says this pointing to the blond male in the picture.

"Yes, it is. Look around you. See! You, have been here before…… It's where you raped her."

I try to say this in as calmer a voice as I can muster.

"Raped who?" He replies quizzically.
"You know who, you quoted Romans 16:16 and you forced yourself on her."

He is clearly a psychopath. He stares blankly at me.   No remorse, nothing. He is one cold bastard.

"Look, I know what the picture shows, but I've honestly never been here before, and certainly never raped anyone. I couldn't, I wouldn't!"

And…. that was it, the anger bubbling within me erupted, and it flooded to the surface. Before I knew it, I had pushed the knife into his chest. I don't even remember getting it from my waistband. It was like I was possessed.

I then start quoting from the Bible myself: 2 Samuel:32, "Surely, you must know this part? After all, we know you love a good biblical quote, especially if it helps you get what you want. For goodness' sake! She was a child; you were a man! …. I am betting you definitely know this one. I bet you know it word for word, don't you! LISTEN TO ME, LISTEN!" …. I'm shouting at this point, and I don't even realise. I want to be heard. The silence which I have had within me, has been kept for too long.

I continue. I had read it so many times that I knew it verbatim. "Only Amnon is dead. This has been Absalom's express intention ever since the day Amnon raped his sister Tamar…."

Fear, instantly flashed in his eyes, and he begins pleading with me. He knew his fate.

"Please! I don't know who you are, or what you want. Look, I have money. Not here, but plenty at home. I have a phone, a car; you can have them. Have all of them."

I had zoned out by this point; I couldn't stand listening to him anymore.... He was a monster and just like David had done with Goliath, I was going to slay him.

I don't remember how many times that I stabbed him. He'd stumbled backwards, and was now on the woodland floor. He was silent but his eyes, they continued to plead with my own.... I ignored them however, as he'd ignored hers, all those years ago....

He didn't fight back. He just clutched where he'd been wounded. Just like a lamb, and not the angry lion that I had expected.... I then finished the job with one swift slit to his throat. It was finally over!

I sat there for a while, tired and processing what I'd just done. He was dead. Then it fully dawned on me. I've bloody well killed him. His eyes were glassy, and there was blood everywhere. On him, on me... I needed to clean up.... I had worn black clothing intentionally. I knew that it would hide most of the blood (if it went that far). And I really was soaked to the skin.

All he had to do was say sorry. I wanted his confession, his remorse, and to know his future intentions. His failure to do those honourable things, they had cost him his life. His actions had earned him his fate... This was karma.

After a very brief consideration of the scene before me, I snapped back into practical mode. I ran to the shed and grabbed the tarpaulin. I tried to roll him on to it.

Blimey, he really was heavy! With some effort, I finally managed it, and I started packaging him up in it. I had some ratchet straps that I was trying to secure my bundle with, but I couldn't get it tight enough. I knew I was under the cover of the wood, but it was still daylight and at any time somebody could come by, and catch me.   My attempts of shifting the body to any great distance were fruitless…. "Right! Plan B."

I ran back and I got the petrol, hammer, and bolt-cutters… and as gruesome as it was, I then proceeded to snip off every fingertip and toe. I then smashed his face in using the hammer. I needed every last one of those pearly whites. I couldn't risk him being identified, and anything coming back to me…

I placed all of the body parts that I had removed into a carrier bag. I would get rid of them later. I did a silent prayer that he didn't have some type of metal plate inserted, that could still identify him.   I knew however that time was not on my side. I had no spare moment to try and investigate further... I just had to hope that he didn't. I then carried on with my tasks...

Almost done. I could imagine the finish line. Then I thought *"Shit, ID!"* I'd almost forgotten to search him. I found his wallet, and a bunch of keys. (A Vauxhall car key, and a set of house keys), also a very basic Nokia mobile phone. I put these to one side, and I made a mental note to look for his car along the lane...

Then, I wrapped him back up as best as I could. Doused him in petrol. Lit the match, and I watched his body become engulfed in the flames. The heat was as intense as my feelings of accomplishment.

Burn in hell, you old bastard! I can't erase the years of pain and suffering that you've caused, but at least I had justice, and he was now punished... The only type of punishment that a man like him deserved...

I stayed briefly to guard my bonfire, but no one came. I'm surprised that no one called the Fire Brigade, or Police. The scene of the crime was like a beacon, with the big billowing clouds of smoke escaping up into the sky.

I relocated to my car. I waited and watched, but no one came...

I then drove home the long way. I'd already gotten changed, before getting into the driver's seat. My blood-stained clothes were wrapped in a polythene bag, along with my trainers, and both were now nestled safely in the boot of my car...

I stopped by the Estuary, and I popped on a pair of latex gloves. I then reached into my grim goodie bag of severed body bits. I scattered them into the water. I retained the bag, putting it back with my clothes. All the while, I was thinking he may as well do something positive and provide a meal for the wildlife. So, there is some good to come out of this, after all!

The keys, wallet and turned off phone I would dispose of later…

Turning back towards home, it felt good. I knew I would have to go back in a few days to check if anything was left; but for now, I was at peace.

I turned up the driveway, the porch light was on. Once I'd parked up, I took a deep breath, and in I went. It was over.

DCI Jo Gordon

She's given her notice. She is going back to the University. They've offered her a part-time teaching position. Apparently, it will fit in better with her family life. She is such a sap. What about her bloody career?!!

To be honest, it's the best news for me. She was so obstructive over that bloody key, and to be frank, I couldn't really work out why. There are probably no forensics on it anyway. It's been in the dirt how long?

***

I'm still waiting on the Council to come back over the car. Apparently, my data protection request form got lost. They are such job-worths! So, I've now got DC Non-Descript on the case, and she's following it up. I don't hold too much hope.

Also, Monroe has been on my case. He has been reminding me that the Bramley Wood job is no longer in my remit, but I just can't let it go.

Scene Examiner Jones

I'm so excited. I've given in my notice. I no longer need that job, and John has agreed to the move. We are just in the process of packing up the house. We've got a buyer, and we have found a wonderful home. It's just that bit bigger, and it will give the girls and us, space to grow.

I'm also going back to the University. A teaching post, but I'm sure in time, I'll get a research project on the side. I'm itching to use my brain again. Managing budgets, and toeing the party line was never really me. I never really felt like I was making a difference, and there was so much stress... especially having Jo as a boss. Does she ever give up?

John has been up in the loft, and he has brought down a load of boxes for me to sort through. He says it's a perfect opportunity for a clear out. I can't really be bothered. There are too many skeletons in the closet for my liking. I'll force myself to have a look later. For now, I must get on with dinner, and I've got an exercise class to get to.

DCI Jo Gordon

I'm at the Local Station again, some debrief that
Monroe wants me to attend...
I'm just coming up the stairs, past the Custody Suite and
I bump into PC Fuller.

"Ah Ma'am, I didn't expect you this quickly. I only left
the voicemail ten minutes, or so ago."
"Voicemail? Fuller, what are you talking about?"
"My voicemail. On your phone."
"Yes, I get the concept of where you leave a voicemail,
Fuller! What did the voicemail say?"
"Well, you know that body in the wood?"
"Yes, Fuller, I know the body in the wood. The one you
urinated on?"
"Yes, Ma'am." *He looks away sheepishly...*
"What about it? Come on Fuller.... Chop, chop!"
"Well, I've just nicked him."

"Have you had a blow to the head Fuller? What are you talking about?"

"Well, the bloke that I've just nicked, he is a dead ringer for him. That mock-up Ma'am… Just come with me."

I do go with him, but only to find out what the bloody hell that he is going on about… I'll just have to be a bit late for Monroe's meeting…

I make my way into Custody, and down the corridor and towards the cells.

"Ma'am, he's here. Cell number 12."

Fuller opens the wicket, and sure enough, I'm looking at the face of a dead man. *What the hell?*

Straight away, I make my way towards the Custody Desk. "Alright, Bob? Number 12? What is he in for, and do we know him?"

Bob Smythe is a seasoned Custody Sergeant. This place is his domain. He looks up, clearly annoyed by my interruption, but he's fully aware that I outrank him.

"Yes Ma'am, and how may I be of assistance?"

"Number 12? Is he known?" My tone clearly expressing my irritation at having to repeat myself, knowing full well that he heard me the first time....

"Mmm, number 12, drink-drive Ma'am, and yes he has a PNC record. Although...." (he pauses) "He's not been nicked since the '70's... Indecent assault."

"Really... What's the result? Does it say?"

Bob taps a few keys and then answers.... "Discontinued, no other details known... Mind you, that would have been on paper records, only the barest minimum of information got put on when we went computerised. I'm surprised we even have as much as that."

PC Fuller then comes up to the desk ... "What do you think Ma'am?"

"I don't know, I just don't know, but I'm going to find out."

I turn away, and I'm just about to leave, when I think to myself...*What's his bloody name?*

I go back to Bob.   He's already looking up at me from his computer... "Yes Ma'am, was there something else?"
"Yes, sorry. What's his name?"
"Number 12?" Bob asks. *I'm sure he does it to annoy me.   Of course, I want to know about number 12!*
"Yes, Bob!" I say in a bit of a huff. "Number 12 please Bob*!" I feel like I'm on a numerical version of bloody Blockbusters!*
"Ah yes, I'll just check" .... *He makes a show of scrolling along his computer screen.* "Here it is, your chap is called... Charlie Jacobs."

Right, Charlie Jacobs, I think to myself.   Who are you? And why are you the exact image of a dead man?

I thank Bob for his assistance, the self-righteous prick that he is, and I exit custody.

Fuller is long gone. He's clearly trying to get his case-file done, so that he can get off home. Poor bugger, I don't blame him, he's already well into the next team's shift. I'll give him his due however, I think he's just given me the break that I needed.

Thank you, PC Fuller, all is <u>almost</u> forgiven!"

Scene Examiner Jones

I'm too tired after my class to start going through the boxes. Instead, I opt for a glass of wine and some trashy TV, whilst I curl up on the sofa next to John.... He has already put the girls to bed. Apparently, they are really excited about the move, and their new bedrooms... Heidi wants a pink room with cloud wallpaper, and Maggie she wants a more "grown-up room" with a "feature wall!" She really makes me laugh that one.... She is definitely older than her years... I had absolutely no idea what a feature wall was at her age....and I'm not entirely sure I know what one is now... all that time watching 'Changing Rooms' with Carol Smillie back in the '90's, was completely wasted on me!

It's half ten by the time I look at the clock, and I'm shattered. I say to John, "Shall we head up?" He nods. I go to the bathroom first; I brush my teeth and wash my face. He's not far behind me, but I don't hear him get into bed. I'm already asleep.

Finally, I feel at peace.

DCI Jo Gordon

DC Non-Descript has chased up the car, and to my amazement, the council still has it. She's on her way down there now with the key. I just hope that it fits. After all, we got nothing from it forensically. I've told her to take along both evidence bags and a log with her. I've got a really good feeling about this. I'm also waiting on the temporary replacement for Shirlie to run Mr Jacobs DNA through the system. I want a familial search, and I'm anxious to see if anything pops up.

Bramley Wood - 2 days after the murder

I've returned to the scene. I drove the scenic route, just to see if I could spot a Vauxhall parked up. But nothing! He did say that he had car trouble, maybe he took a train or got a cab? I walk into the clearing. I've brought a shovel with me. My plan is to dig a grave and then push whatever that is left into it...

I approach the body, there is not much thankfully that still remains, and It's only just about recognisable as human. I dig a trench next to it, and then scrape him into it. I then cover that over with some soil, leaves, and loose branches. I only really do this to camouflage the fact that the ground has been freshly dug. I then go back to my car. I still need to get rid of my clothes, and his personal effects. I feel a garden bonfire is in order. I've been clearing a number of tree branches at home. No one will suspect a thing.

DCI Jo Gordon.

DC Non-Descript has come up trumps. I really should learn her bloody name, but anyway she calls me. I can hear the excitement in her voice.

"Ma'am!" she says... "I think I've got something!"

I nearly pissed my pants when she told me, and I could hardly believe my ears... It turned out, that in that innocuous little old car, that was sat for months near the entrance to the wood, and then picked up by the Council. It held a vital piece of evidence. Thank the Lord, for that meddling "Old Dear" who had called us by mistake, to report that it was making the area look untidy! If she hadn't, it could have been removed and we would have never even known of its existence... That little old car was on the Council's list for destruction, AND was very nearly crushed! Boy! I'm glad we got to it first! Jackpot! I've got them... The car was a winner! I knew it would be.

That evidence could have been so easily missed, but thankfully it wasn't! It's a little piece of paper; a scribbled address, and a map to the scene of the murder. And even more importantly, it has the name and address of whom the vehicle's driver was meeting that day....

I followed up on the deceased car owner's final address, (as I had nothing more to go on). I got a search warrant, and arranged for Local Officers to attend, and to my surprise, there were pictures and correspondence for a Colin Joseph... And here's the amazing part. When they emailed over the images of what they had found, the photographs at the residence, showed that Mr Joseph is also a dead ringer for Mr Jacobs. Fuller's drink-drive, who had now almost sobered up in the cells.

I have also got Graham on the case, re-examining the bones from the Wood. I want to see if anything was missed. I am pretty sure that he will somehow find something that will help me tie this whole case together.

There is no time to lose, I know who I need to speak to. I can't believe that my number one suspect was right under my nose all along.

I'm coming for you!

Scene Examiner Jones

I have had the most amazing of sleeps. I am not sure if it's because I no longer have to go back to that place, or because of the imminent house move, but right now I feel great.

I was so grateful to HR when I put in my resignation, as they had advised that due to holiday owed, I didn't need to work my notice period. Graham had snapped my hand off when I asked if he had wanted to cover my role temporarily. To be honest, I think he was a little put out when I first took it on. I still can't believe it, I managed nearly three years at that place... but he had always seen the job as his, and now it was.

Today I feel refreshed, and I'm ready to tackle those boxes.

I've eaten my breakfast, and I'm just finishing off my coffee when John walks into the kitchen. We're both on rest days (me, permanently until I start back at the University). He had left me sleeping in, whilst he got the girls up and ready, and he took them to school. He really is a keeper!

"Shall we sort these boxes then?" ...I say gesturing towards them over on the counter.
"Yes, come on then."

I move the first one and open it. It's an old Volvic Mineral Water box. It has white with blue writing on it, with some sort of mountainous scene. It looks out of place amongst the other brown generic packing boxes. I don't even remember seeing it before.

"What's this one?" I ask.

"I don't know darling!" … John replies, a little irritated already. I know he hates household chores, but this was his idea!

I start to open it. And after pulling back only one-half of the box's flaps, I instantly know what it is. "What's this doing here?" My voice is shaky.

"Oh, I remember, it's from your mum. She brought it ages ago. Bits from your childhood. I had popped it in the loft for safekeeping."

"And …. Did you look at any of it?" I say this a little harsher than I'd meant to.

He looks over at me, he has so much love in his eyes.

"I'm sorry darling, but I did, yes."

"So, you know?"

He nods his head to confirm my worst fears. My secret, the thing that has defined my whole adult life. He knows about it, and I wasn't the one to tell him. Well, how could I? It's not the thing that you can easily slip into a conversation. "Pass me the salt darling, and oh yes, and by the way, did I tell you... Oh, and I have a really interesting fact, I'm the product of...." No, he was never meant to know. No one was. Why would Mum bring that here? I just don't understand?

"How long? How long have you known?"
"A while, Baby. I found out not long after we moved in here. Your mum brought over the box and I was intrigued. At first, I wasn't sure what I had stumbled across. I had thought that it was you, but then not wanting to cause any upset, I asked your mum, and she filled me in. It doesn't matter, Baby, it's all in the past."

I collapse in his arms and I start to sob. The hurt and angst that I had kept in, kept hidden, it instantly came flooding out.

Then I'm startled, there's a knock at the door. A really heavy knock at the door. I turn, and see through the glass window of the front door and porch, that there are flashing blue lights….

I unpeeled myself from John, who seemed to be hugging me even closer than before. I go over to the door and open it.

It's Jo, she is stood staring at me. Her eyes are cold. She then opens her mouth and says…. "Dr Michelle Jones, I'm arresting you for the murder of Colin Joseph. You do not have to say anything, but it may harm your defence if you do not mention when questioned, something that you later rely on in court, and anything you do say may be given in evidence. Your arrest is necessary for the preservation of evidence, and so we can get your account on taped interview."

She is so formal in her delivery, and then my mind, it registers what she has just said. "MURDER!"

"Take her away!" Jo says, and I am then cuffed and led out to a police van. I can see that the neighbour's curtains are twitching. What is happening to me? A female officer then pats me down. She is in uniform, and she can't be much older than 18, 19 years of age. Her face is empty. She's got on the same blue examination gloves, that had become part of my daily wardrobe. It all seems so clinical, so cold. Then I'm helped up into the back of the van, and I'm placed in the cage. The door is shut and then nothing. It's silent; the stale and musty air within, it hangs heavy and is suffocating.

The next thing I hear, is a muffled male voice. "You had better get in the back Meg, best to watch her. You never know what she might get up to." Then the same female officer slides open the side door of the van, and she sits on the lone seat in the rear, staring back at me.

John

Shit, Shit! She has been arrested, and now they are ransacking our home. I feel so hopeless. What can I do?

Why on earth wasn't I warned? Surely, someone from my old team knew about this before old Big Boots rocked up. Shit, shit! Why didn't they tell me?

My next thought is the girls. What am I going to say to them? I never dreamed they'd arrest her. Why would they? Surely, they know her? Surely even Jo can see that she'd never hurt anyone? It's not in her nature. Jo, on the other hand, she does it on a regular basis. Stepping over, and even on people if it suits her need. She's a heartless cow!

I call her Mum. I can hear the shock in her voice, but she straight away, and without hesitation says "I'll sort out the girls. You've got nothing to worry about there. I'll be over in a jiffy." She then pauses, and with a deep intake of breath she says, "John, what evidence have they got?"

"How should I know?" My reply is a little tart, and I certainly didn't mean anything by it, but I really didn't know. The only thing that I was sure of, was that I needed to get her a legal rep, and a good one at that.

I considered my options very briefly, and although it went totally against the grain, I knew that there was only one person for this job, and that man was Larry King.

Larry was an ex-DCI; and after his 30 years' service, rather than do what most retirees do, when they are not quite ready to let go of the institution. They still bin their public-order boots, and instead they choose to stay on in a civilian role. You know, the usual shite of filing reports, and doing the admin, etc. Oh no, not him!

Not Larry! No! He broke the mould, he retrained. He joined the other side, and he became legal counsel for the defence.

Talk about poacher, turned gamekeeper.

He was however, the best. He knew all about police tactics and policy. It was second nature, and if anyone was going to help me and her to sort this mess out, it had to be him.

I pull up the internet on my phone, and I search for his number. Bingo! His firm is the first hit on Google.

Scene Examiner Jones

We drive no longer than 20-30 minutes, and I can feel the cold air in the back of the van. I had only worn lightweight clothing, as I wasn't really expecting to go out today. Well, other than to do the school run later, but I would definitely have popped on a jumper, before leaving the house. It certainly wasn't the hazy, warm spring day that I had been expecting, when the sun had woken me up this morning. I wasn't sure if it was the shock of being arrested, or simply that I hadn't dressed appropriately, but I felt chilled to the bone. And to be honest, how in all reality do you really dress for being arrested? It's hardly something that you can anticipate. Especially when you're not a hardened criminal.

I hear the female officer's voice; she is speaking on her radio, and she asks for the gates to be opened. We must have arrived at the Station. We slow slightly turning to the left as we draw into the yard. We drive on but only for a few feet, and then I feel the van judder back and forth, as it tries to locate its place in the jigsaw puzzle of vehicles, that is a police backyard.

The engine is turned off, then there is silence. The male officer jumps out of the van. I know this, as I can feel the weight distribution shift briefly. He then comes to the side door and slides it open. My senses are heightened as I hear him say, "Meg, you stay there and watch her. I'll go and see how many there are ahead of us. Hopefully, they will give us special treatment, seeing as it's one of our own. The less that see her, the better. I doubt Ma'am will want the press to get hold of this one just yet!"

I sit there looking at PC Megan through the Perspex window, that is separating us. She is sat there completely blank-faced. No eye contact, no nothing. It's like she is void of anything. She is certainly not going to be making any small talk with me.

The wait for him to return feels like hours, but it's only probably 15-20 minutes at max. The rear door is flung open. It's the male police officer who had chauffeured us here. He smells of cigarettes. He has clearly had a crafty fag, on route back to us. "Right, out you get…. Sarge is ready for us…"

I'm led into the Custody Suite, flanked by PC Megan and this male officer, (I am yet to discover his name). His epaulette is missing one of his numbers, so I can't even identify him for later on, when I'm looking to name him and the others, in my unlawful arrest complaint to the IOPC (Independent Office for Police Conduct.) This whole pantomime is absolutely outrageous!

Once inside, what hits me first is the smell. Believe it or not, but in my relatively brief career within the Force, I have never yet been into a Custody Suite. The smell is a nausea-inducing cocktail of cannabis, an air freshener, which is some sort of synthetic peach smell; English fry ups and faeces. It's absolutely hideous, and these officers work here daily! Often 12-hour shifts at a time. No wonder that their judgement is sometimes off! It must really mess with your head; I tell you; it's messing with mine, and I've been here what? 30 seconds?

I'm led to a desk area, which is located in the middle of the Custody Suite. It is raised to standing height, and there is a rather skinny, grey-haired man, sat the other side. He looks weary, and he is currently peering over his dark-rimmed glasses at me.

"Right then Officer, tell me the facts of the offence."

PC Megan speaks. It's the first time that I have heard her voice properly (bar her asking for the gates to be opened). "Sarge, I'm booking in on behalf of Ma'am Gordon. She's still at the scene. The arrest was made at 09:45 hours this morning, and the relevant time is 10:38

hours." I find out later that the relevant time is simply the time that we arrived at the Police Station. It has some bearing on the PACE clock, and apparently, it is quite important.

"She's been arrested for the murder of Colin Joseph on 25th April 2018, up at BRAMLEY WOOD. She's been arrested for a prompt and effective investigation, and for the preservation of evidence."
"Any reply to caution?" He asks her.
"Um, I don't think so Sarge, no, nothing."
"Any significant statements?"
"No Sarge, she's not said a word."

They talk about me as if I'm not even there, and to be honest, I really wish I wasn't.

The Sergeant carries on with his questions...

"Warrant number?"

"Sorry Sarge, I don't know Ma'am's, but mine is 251041."

"Ok, I'll look hers up, not a problem Constable.   You must be fresh out the box, with a 25 at the start!" ... He says smiling at himself, but I haven't got a clue what he's talking about!

The Sergeant is typing furiously, but I'm not exactly sure what he's actually writing up. He then briefly looks up and says "Murder aye, I see.... And was she cuffed?"

"Yes Sarge, still is."

"Well, do we think we could remove them now, Constable?"

There is an air of annoyance in the Sergeant's voice, and in his delivery. I wondered if PC Megan had broken protocol, by making me wear them for so long? Another thing for me to find out for my complaint. My cuffs, they are removed, and the Sergeant takes a note of their unique serial number. He begins to check my wrists for injuries. There are none.

PC Megan is then asked if she searched me. She confirms that she has, but he still gets her to search me again. On go those blue gloves, and I am patted down. She is much more thorough than before. It's quite degrading as she moves the back of her palm, up and around my groin. What is she expecting to find? I'm only wearing lightweight cotton trousers, and you can clearly see that I've not got anything concealed. She then does the same on my top half, lingering around my bra. She then gets a black bat-shaped thing, and moves this across me too. It beeps, but she confirms to the Sergeant that it's just due to the under-wires.

I am then told to remove my jewellery. My beautiful trilogy engagement ring that John bought me all those years ago. My eternity ring, AKA my push present from when Maggie was born… I consider this for a moment, as I'm still waiting for the one from Heidi's birth. I think that John must have forgotten. I'll have to remind him once this charade is all over. I also have to take off my wedding band. This greatly saddens me, as I have never once removed it, since John had put it on my finger on our wedding day. I do query this, but the Sergeant is very insistent. "Everything Off! You'll get it back, but you can't take anything of value into the cells."

They also take my Fitbit off. That funnily enough, stresses me out more than the rings. How am I going to track my steps? I have nothing else on me, so I sign an electronic pad, confirming that they have taken all of my belongings. They are now contained in a sealed plastic bag that PC Megan had been writing on.

I stand there whilst he asks me a series of questions. He takes my personal information, and then he queries my wellbeing. Name, address, medication, next of kin, any suicidal thoughts, etc... He then beckons over a young lad, and instructs him to 'process me'. This simply means taking my photo, fingerprints, and a DNA swab. I feel so violated.

I am then led down the long corridor to my cell. There is a toilet in the corner, a concrete bed with a blue thin mattress, and I'm told that they will get me a blanket in a while. I think even they can work out that I'm freezing. My arms are mottled, I have goose pimples, and my hairs are standing up on end. I can also feel that my nipples are rock hard, and will no doubt be poking through my thin material top. A perk for the young Detention Officer, as he clearly fails to look away, when I catch his obvious stare. He advises me to press the buzzer if I need anything, but he also tells me to be mindful. They are busy, and this is a Police Custody and not a hotel. With that, he shuts my cell door, and then I hear the slam of the wicket. I am all alone.

I sit down on the bed, and the plastic-covered mattress, it creaks underneath me. Reality hits like a sledgehammer. What the hell has just happened? Murder?

DCI Jo Gordon

I have directed the search at the house. I want any paperwork that they can find that has any connection to the deceased. I also want electrical items; laptops, tablets, etc. as well as any mobile phones. I want that burner phone. I want to know how she made contact.

I'm alerted to the rear garden. One of the search officers has seen that there is a garden incinerator. John is still at the house, and he observes the officer pointing it out.

"You won't find anything there, Jo! Or anywhere else for that matter! Geez, you really are grasping at straws! Do you have any actual bloody evidence?"
"Look, do you have somewhere else that you can go? If you stay here, you are at risk of being arrested for obstruction. You are preventing my officers from carrying out their lawful duty!"

"Oh, piss off you bitch! Lawful duty? This is a bloody witch-hunt and you know it!"

"I know nothing of the sort, this is all built on credible evidence..."

I take a breath and I stop myself. In my anger, I nearly gave disclosure, and that's the last thing that I want to do. Well…. Not to the husband anyway and definitely not to John. I walk away, and I carry-on directing the officers in their search.

I also ensure that John is not left on his own. He seems very interested in staying in the kitchen. What is he hiding? His phone rings, and he goes just outside of the front door to take it. It must be important, as he clearly doesn't want me to hear.

After the call, he comes back to the kitchen, and over to where there is a stack of boxes. I've got uniform going through them. He looks worried, but then he turns to me, "Look, I've got to go. You'll find nothing. She didn't do it!"

With that, he has manoeuvred his 4x4, past all the police vehicles and he's gone. *Bugger!* I think. I wanted that searched. Then, however, I remembered how particular John was in relation to his cars. Only HE gets to drive them. So, unless he's had a very recent personality transplant, I very much doubt that she would have had any access to his precious vehicle; let alone used it in the planning and execution of her bloody crime.

I leave the search team to it, as I only really stayed to keep an eye on John. I then see that two of my DC's have arrived. I make my way over to them, doing the necessary pleasantries, and I direct them to make door to door enquiries.

I still feel rather rushed. That crucial discovery that DC Non-Descript made, less than 24 hours ago had forced me to speed up this part of the investigation. I had to beg, borrow and steal team officers to help with the arrest, and even the search team are here on a rather tenuous favour. I could hear it in Monroe's voice when I made the call. He was pleased that I had made a breakthrough. However, due to the need for speed, he unfortunately, couldn't give me my old team. They were committed elsewhere on another op, and as gutted as I was, I just couldn't take the risk that some do-gooder; some mate of John's wouldn't tip him off, and any evidence that might still be around; lost.

No, it wasn't as smooth as I'd hoped, but at least I had her in Custody. Her place was being turned-over, and soon I'd be doing what I did best. With this thought in mind, I got back into my car and I left them to it. I made my way to the Station. I had a very important interview to prepare for.

Scene Examiner Jones

Eventually, they bring me my blanket. It's rough to the touch but it actually smells clean. It's the only thing in this whole place that does. I also requested a cup of tea. I just needed something that would help me to warm up. It was O.K. Not my usual brew, and a little stronger than I normally took it, but I didn't complain. The young detention officer's words "This is not a hotel!" kept going around in my head, and I really didn't want to piss him off. I thought rather wisely, that due to the predicament that I was in, I needed as many brownie points as possible, and annoying my captors was not something I thought I should do. Well, not by complaining about something as innocuous as the strength of a cuppa.

The skinny and grey-haired Sergeant had been to see me. He had opened the wicket, and asked me if I had wanted legal advice. When I was being booked in, I wasn't sure, but after being locked up in this windowless small box, it had focused my mind. Yes, I definitely needed the help of a professional.

"Duty, or do you have your own?" He asked.
"Duty, I suppose, I don't have my own."
"Righty-oh!" He replied... and then he was gone, slamming the wicket shut again as he left. I was then back to the enclosed and stale air of the cell, and the unnerving and deafening silence.

My stomach, it began to twist and turn. I could feel my chest tightening. I then began to think about my girls. My beautiful girls. What was John going to tell them when they came home from school, and Mummy wasn't there? They already knew that I'd left the Police, and that I had some time off planned before starting my new job. Maggie had excitedly hugged me when I'd told them. "Oh Mummy, we can have so much fun before you go back to work." I've already failed her. I'm not even going to be there when she's home tonight. I feel even worse as I picture her disappointed little face.

I hardly think that this is going to be a five minute, in and out job either. It's not like I had forgotten to pay for a bag of oranges. Not like poor Hannah. She'd left them hung on the trolley, and then walked out of the shop.... I still couldn't believe it. They arrested her! A probationer according to John! "No discretion darling, not when you're learning."

Poor, poor Hannah! Baby brain had managed to get her a Police Caution for shoplifting!

I wonder if you can actually get a caution for murder? I am of course being silly, but your mind wanders off when you don't really know what to do. Can you really be charged for something that you haven't done? You see it all of the time in the movies. The suspect is framed, or there is a miscarriage of justice. A great plot, but how often does it happen in real life? For the whole of my adult life, I've been immersed in science. If there is no scientific link, no evidence that I did this, then how can she really think that I did? I go back to mulling over his name; Colin Joseph and then it twigs. Of course, CJ!

DCI Jo Gordon

John clearly thinks that she has done it! He must do.
He's only gone and got Larry King to represent her.
He'd have only done that, if he thought that she was
guilty. He despises the man almost as much as I do!
That's the only thing these days, that we really do agree
on.

Larry is a bastard. He's only in it for the money. How
can you devote most of your working life to catching the
bad guys, and having them brought to justice, to only
then dedicate your time, to getting them off in
retirement? It makes no sense. No sense at all. It has
to be about the money. Maybe he is a gambler and has
a debt to pay off? It's certainly not to fund a young
wife.... From what I last heard, he is still with that
battle-axe, Helen. She is still in the job. I bet there are
some interesting conversations had around that dinner

table. Talk about a conflict of interest. If he was mine, I'd kill him! Figuratively speaking of course!

Anyway, I digress. Back to the job at hand. I've been called by Custody. Larry has just arrived and I best get going.

John

It felt wrong googling his firm, but I knew that I needed him. You should have heard his tone when the receptionist had transferred the call....

"John! To what do I owe the pleasure? I thought I was off "the list" since I swapped sides?"

"Look, Larry, I need your help."

"My help? What are you on? 'Millionaire?" He says this with a chuckle, "Am I your phone a friend?"

"Yes, something like that. If you can help me, you can pretty much name your price."

"Go on then, I'm listening."

I explained my predicament. "Right, where is she?"

"Central, I think."

"Right, ok, I'm on my way. It's been a while since I've gone toe to toe with Gordon. I'm going to enjoy this."

"Yes, ok Larry. Don't enjoy yourself too much, and don't forget what's at stake here."

"No Mate, I won't. I'll keep you informed."

Mate? I think to myself...well, he is now. I would have made a deal with the devil just to help her. In fact, I realise that I just have!

The call is ended, and I'm back looking at my phone's wallpaper picture. It's my girls, all three of them – smiling back at me. If I needed a reminder of what was at stake, it was this. My family.

DCI Jo Gordon

Larry King swaggers into the Custody Suite. He still acts as if it's his domain. He forgets that he is only a guest these days. He is here on invitation. Not by me, I might add. He is a toxic little prick!

He is busy chatting with Bob from across the Suite. I don't know why they tolerate him. He's talking about his handicap, and that they must sort out a game soon. Unbelievable! I thought he was here for a job, and not to sort out a social!

"Hello, Detective Chief Inspector Gordon. How are we? Are those big boots fitting any better?"

He really does rate himself.

"Right, I have just seen my client, and we have done the introductions. She is a lovely wee lass, and happily

married to John Jones. I believe you pair once dated?"
He says this grinning at me, and trying to provoke a
reaction no doubt. Well, he is not getting one.

"Room three is free, if you're ready for disclosure?" I
say this slightly more officiously than I meant to.
"Ouch! Touched a nerve, have I?"

I really want to tell him to bugger off, but I'm not going
to let him derail this investigation. Too much is at stake.

Scene Examiner Jones

According to Larry; who is now my legal rep, (John sorted him out for me) it was too risky relying on a duty solicitor for this type of case. So, he is here to provide me with the best possible advice.

Also, they have not let me speak to John, so I have absolutely no idea how the girls are. And it's killing me.

Larry says that the whole case that they have against me started with a key. It was the one that the dog walker found. Even though it came to light months after the discovery of the body. It was the key to a car that was originally located near to the scene. This car apparently contained some documentation that listed me, as who the victim was intending to meet on the day of his death.

Well, if that's all they've got, I don't think I'll be here too long.

"Right then, are you ready for this? And remember what I said, they've got nothing. Let's not give them anything else. So other than saying your name, and confirming that you understand the caution. It's 'no comment' to everything else. Got it?"
"Got it," I say.

Larry pops his head around the interview room door. "Jo, we're ready for you."

DCI Jo Gordon

We walk into the Interview Room. Shirlie and Larry are sat behind the desk. There are two seats opposite them; one for me and the other for DC Non-Descript. Her actual name, which I have now learnt is DC Rachel Cooper.

I would normally have a Detective Sergeant as my second in command, but I felt it was only right to let DC Cooper sit in. After all, she has got to learn, and without her having gone to the Pound, and realising the significance of that paperwork, we wouldn't even be here. Credit, where credit is due, I always say!

"Ok… Shall we get started?" I begin by unwrapping the CDs. Two copies. One gets sealed, and the other will be the working copy. I then start with the formalities… "Are you, ok?" I direct this to Shirlie. "Do you need a drink? Have you been to the bathroom?"

She smiles, looking directly at me, and replies that no she is fine. Don't get me wrong, I couldn't give a rat's arse if she's thirsty, or needs to go to the loo, but I'm not letting any technicality get in the way of this case; like overlooking her bloody human rights!

I press the record button and there it is, that comforting and familiar long tone that signals the start of round one! (DING DING!)

"Ok then. It's Wednesday 15th May 2019 and the time by my watch is 20:38 hours, the location is Central Police Station, Interview Room 3. I'm DCI Jo Gordon. Also, in the room is..."

I signal to DC Cooper.

"DC Cooper." She states this for the tape.

"This is a taped interview concerning; please state your name and date of birth for the tape..."

I signal to Shirlie and she says...

"Dr Michelle Jones, I'm not exactly sure of my actual date of birth, but I was given 24th February 1980."

"Ok thank you, also in the room is."

Larry needs no such signal, he's straight in with...

"Larry King from King Associates, acting as legal representation."

"Ok, I must remind you that you are still under caution. You do not have to say anything, but it may harm your defence if you do not mention when questioned, something that you later rely on in court, and anything you do say may be given in evidence. Do you understand?"

Shirlie nods.

"For the tape, please. The suspect has just nodded her head."

"Oh, yes, sorry. I understand."

"Ok perfect, let us begin. Ok, so you...sorry, what do you want me to call you?"

I say this looking directly at Shirlie. "Dr Jones, Michelle, or Shelley?"

She looks up at me smiling again. "Erm... Shelley is fine."

"Ok Shelley, you were arrested earlier today for the murder of Colin Joseph on 25th April 2018 at Bramley Wood. Please can you tell me your side of the story?" She looks at Larry. He shakes his head and taps the paperwork that he has in front of him. With my eyes straining, I can just about see what it says. It's large capital letters. I make out "N C." Of course, he's advised her to go "no comment." As soon as I've realised this, she replies as expected.

"No comment."

"Can you tell me where you were in the afternoon of 25th April 2018?"

"No comment."

Oh God.... this is going to be boring. I know she is going to go "no comment" to every single question that I put to her... I ask her how she knows Colin Joseph, who he is to her? How long she has known him for? .... And after each question that I pose, she looks to Larry for guidance. Each and every time, he taps his paper and she utters her guided response of "no comment."

I showed her the paperwork found in the car, and I asked her if she recognised it. I could tell that she did as her blue eyes briefly sparked.   It was from a DNA Ancestry Database Company called Entwined. In it, it showed a 99.99% parentage link between her and the deceased, Colin Joseph. I could see it dawning on her that she was in very deep water.

"I'm showing you exhibit REC/01.   It is paperwork that was found in Mr Joseph's deceased father's car. Can you explain it to me…? And how you appear to be the biological daughter of Joseph?"
"No comment."
"Scribbled in the corner of this document is a mobile number of 07989325228. Can you tell me if you recognise this number?"
"No comment."

"We already know that it's a burner phone. Is it your burner phone?"

"No comment."

"Where is this phone?"

"No comment."

"Subscriber checks show that it was in regular communication with Mr Joseph from February 2018 to April 2018. Was that you? Were you using it to communicate with Joseph?"

"No comment."

There is a knock on the door. *For goodness' sake!* I think to myself. *What do they want?*

"Enter," I say, my tone not masking my annoyance. I was on a roll, knocking down her defences one by one...

"For the tape, DS Pick has entered the room."

I look down at what he has just given to me. I am trying really hard to maintain my poker face. DS Pick then leaves the room.

"For the purpose of the tape, DS Pick has just given me some relevant information, and he has now left the room." Talking directly at Shirlie, I say "Would you like me to suspend the interview, to provide further disclosure to your Legal Rep?"

Again, she looks at Larry…. He shakes his head and taps a different part of the pad. He then circles something with his pen. It's written again in block handwriting. I can just about make out TICS. The stupid, arrogant, git! He clearly thinks that was a ploy just to unnerve her. Of course! POLICE TACTICS!

She answers, "No, it's fine." But her voice is quivering. She is clearly unnerved.
"Ok then, if you're sure?"

"I'm showing you exhibits MA/3 and TWE/14. Can you look at both of these pictures? MA/3 is a polaroid image, it shows two men. There is writing at the bottom of the image. It says Barnaby and CJ. Have you seen this image before?"

"No comment."

"It was found at your home, in what appeared to be packing boxes. Can you explain how it came to be there?"

"No comment."

"Ok Shelley, what about this image? For the tape, I'm showing exhibit TWE/14, can you take a look? This was found during a search at the victim's address."

Shirlie pulls it towards her and she carefully studies the image.

"Good, I'm glad you had a good look. Would you say that the male to the right of the image on the polaroid, is the same male in the other image? Wouldn't you say that they were one in the same? That image, exhibited as TWE/14 is Colin Joseph!" *I pause for effect* "So I say again. How do you know him? You must…. Otherwise, why would you have a photo of him at your home address?"

"No comment."

"Ok, let's go back to the day in question. I've asked you where you were on Wednesday 25th April 2018. You've elected as is your right, to answer 'no comment'. However, I have a statement here that DS Pick has just brought in to me. It's from a neighbour of yours. A Jeanette Burns, she lives next door, is that right?"

"No comment."

"Well, this is interesting reading…. Jeanette… she advises that she remembers the afternoon of Wednesday 25 April 2018, really rather well. You see, it says here she'd only just got back from France, and she had popped over to visit you at your home address. Apparently, you had called her a lifesaver. Why would you call her that?"

"No comment. "

"Was it because she enabled you to go and meet Mr Joseph, and for you to carry out your plan of killing him? Not much of a lifesaver, is she?"

"No comment."

"Now, apparently, she babysat your two girls; Maggie and Heidi, is it?"

"No comment."

I can see that I have touched a nerve. That last no comment was through gritted teeth. *Am I getting to you Shirlie-dear?* I continue.

"So, Jeanette, she said it was so that you could go to your fitness class. Was that right?"

"No comment."

"Well, we checked at the local gym, and yes you were down to attend, but you were marked as a no show. Can you explain this?"

"No comment."

"Now, here is the really interesting bit; Mrs Burns, she says that you arrived back home approximately 2 hours after you'd left. And that you had changed clothes, and that she distinctly remembers that you smelt of Bonfire. Can you explain that to me?"

"No comment." Shirley shifts uncomfortably in her seat. She looks at Larry.

He just gives her a reassuring glance. *I do not get his gameplan, why doesn't he just let her explain? She clearly wants to if her body language is anything to go by!*

I glance down at the statement. DS Pick had highlighted an earlier section that I had initially missed.

"It also says here, that she remembered smelling petrol in your hallway just before you left for your 'class'. Was all of this premeditated? Did you take the petrol with you that day? Was it all part of your plan? Using an accelerant to dispose of the body? After all, as you are well aware, the body that we discovered was burned."

"No comment."

Shirley is looking more and more distressed. I think I've got her. *You're on the ropes lady!*

She looks up at me, she is clearly exhausted and says "I think I need a break."

"Yes ok, no problem. Interview paused at 21:05 hours."

Scene Examiner Jones

Jo leaves the Interview Room, along with her DC sidekick. I don't really see why she's even in here. She's not said a word and we all know that this charade is the "Jo Show!"

I look at Larry. He smiles back at me. "Are you, ok?" "No, not really. Are you really sure that "no comment" is the way to go? Look, I have answers for all of those questions, and every one of them will prove that I didn't do it. Please, can't you just find out what evidence she has? If there's anything additional? And why can't I just answer her questions?"

"Look, Shelley, you are my client, my boss; so, I am directed by you, but in these cases, when the Police have nothing, it's just better to give them nix. It stops them tripping you up…. Look, I should know! I did this job for thirty-odd years. I liked nothing more than finding my "in" with a suspect, and then watching their story begin to crumble.   I'd tear it down brick by brick. Jo is no pussy cat, and I would never tell her this to her face, but she's bloody brilliant! You don't want to go up against her."

"Well, what can I do? It looks like I've got something to hide."

"Well, have you?" Larry looks back at me intently.

I snap, "No! Why would you even ask that?"

"Is that why John sent you? He thinks I'm guilty, so he sent you to get me off? Oh, for God's sake, if even he is not in my corner, what hope have I got?"

My chest begins to tighten, my breathing shallow, and I recognise what it is immediately. I'm having a panic attack.

"Look, calm down Shelley. Have this." Larry passes me a cup of water. It's freezing cold, and it has the desired effect of shocking me out of it.

"Ok I'll ask her for further disclosure, and then we can have another chat. How about we think about a prepared statement?"

"What's that then?"

I am almost back to full composure, other than the metallic taste in my mouth.   I just can't shake it.   I've drunk tea and water, but it still remains. I've had it since my arrest. It's got to be caused by the underlying anxiety. My body's way of dealing with all this stress. Either that, or there is some kind of toxin in the water here.   *Truth serum?* I smile at my absolute randomness…. *Toxins, drugging me?* Of course, it's the bloody anxiety.   It's not exactly a run of the mill day for me, or anyone else for that matter!

I can feel Larry staring at me.

"Hey, are you, ok? You disappeared for a second. Right, shall we carry on? You were asking about a prepared statement?"

"Oh yes..."

"Well, it is as it sounds. You give a written explanation. You'll date and sign it and I'll read it out. She can then ask her questions, but she'll have had her response from you already. Anything further we can 'no comment', but if this does go to court...." I interrupt him in full flow... "What? You.... you actually think this will go to court? You think... I'll get charged?"

"Woah! Look, calm down! Let me finish. IF this does go to court, they can't draw any inferences, as we have provided an explanation at our very first opportunity."

"So, you think this might go to court?" *I'm getting irritated that I have had to repeat the question again, as he didn't answer me the first time. What is he, a bloody politician?*

"Right, let me speak to Jo, and let's see what she's willing to give us... ok?"

"Ok," I say.

"In fact, thinking about it, do you want to go into a rest period? You are entitled to it under PACE."

"No, let's get this over with."

"Ok, you're the boss."

Larry pops his head out of the door and Jo comes over.

"Are we good to go?" She enquires.

"No actually, I think I'll take you up on that additional disclosure."

"Yep, no problem. Shall we go next door? It's free. I'll just get Rachel to sit with the suspect."

Suspect!? She is so cold. A few weeks ago, we were friends (well, sort of). We'd drifted to colleague status, but only very recently. Everything has changed since this bloody case. In fact, the night before Joseph, or whatever his name is, was found, we'd been out drinking. I remember the hangover, and the fact that I

was trying not to vomit at the crime scene! I'm just
pondering this as Larry leaves and DC Rachel comes in
to babysit me.

"Are you ok?" She says. "Do you want a cuppa?" I can
get one of the gaolers to make you one."
I nod. "Actually, that would be lovely. It will help me
get rid of this taste in my mouth."
"How do you take your tea then?"
"As it comes." I was thinking back to the previous
strong brew, but I didn't say anything …   She smiles
back at me and asks….
"Milk, sugar?"
"Oh yes, white without, thank you."

DC Rachel shoves her head out of the door and I hear
her shout.

"Oi Billy, do me a favour, will you…? Make mine a tea,
please? White, without."

I can instantly hear him grumble and say something about a hotel. It must be his stock phrase! She closes the door, and she sits back in the seat opposite the empty one where Larry had been sitting.

"Sorry, I know this is a bit personal, but do you need the toilet? It's been a while, and I thought you might?"
"No thank you," I say. "I'm fine. I think in a past life I was a camel!" I say this with a smile.

She laughs at this just as there is a knock at the door and in comes my tea. Brought in by the lad who had put me in the cell. The one whose eyes I had previously felt staring at my chest!

"Cheers Bill." She says. Well, at least I now know his name.

A few minutes later Larry is back, and DC Rachel is gone... it's just like a revolving door!

"Right then, Disclosure! So, we know about the paperwork from Entwined and the two photos. There is also the statement from your neighbour. The only new stuff is that they have run your DNA, and a toothbrush that they found at the victim's address. It appears that you are related. They also have a calendar from there, which has the date that he supposedly met you on. It shows the location as Bramley Wood, and 16:40 hours is circled in red. So, it suggests that was the time you agreed to meet."

"But I didn't meet him... it wasn't me!   What do we do? Do I answer her questions, or do this prepared statement thingy?"

"I think we go for a prepared statement. It's our safest option. Anyway, I wouldn't put it past her to hold something back. She is well known for liking a well-stocked arsenal."

"Ok then, let's do it."

It takes a further 30 minutes to get everything down in the statement. I've told Larry everything. It feels right, and I'm much happier giving an explanation, rather than the endless "no commenting" that I've done up until now.

"Right, sign, and date here. This will become your exhibit, so MJ/1."

Larry writes this in the top corner of the lined sheets, where he's scribbled down my explanation to this whole sorry affair.

"Are you ready? Need a wee, anything?" *I really don't know why everyone is so obsessed with my bladder!*

"No, no, I'm fine. Let's get this done."
"Okey-dokey."

Larry puts his head out of the door, and within seconds DC Rachel and DCI Gordon are back in the room.

DCI Jo Gordon

I switch on the recorder....

"Interview resumed, it's still Wednesday 15th May 2019, and the time is 22:35 hours.   I am DCI Jo Gordon, also in the room is...." Gesturing to Rachel.

"DC Rachel Cooper."

"And this interview is a continuation of the earlier interview with..." I gesture towards Shirlie. "Dr Michelle Jones."

"Also, in the room is" ...*Larry* is straight in there again, no gesturing required.... "Larry King, Legal representation."

"Ok then, we'll get started again, shall we? ... I must remind you that you are still under caution. To refresh your memory..."   *The caution is repeated.*

"Do you understand?"

"Yes," Shirlie replies.

"Ok then, where were we?" I'm looking down at my notes, and I'm ready to ask my next question when Larry interrupts me.

"DCI Gordon, my client has instructed me to provide a prepared statement. I'll read it now and she exhibits it as MJ/1."

I look over at the scribbled mess of whatever bullshit that they have clearly decided to run with.

"Go ahead, Larry," I say with a smile. *This is going to be interesting.*

Larry clears his throat and begins to speak:

"I, Dr Michelle Jones, make this statement in relation to my arrest for the murder of Colin Joseph. I am aware this may be used in evidence if this goes to court. I wish to advise that I do not know, nor

have I ever met Mr Joseph. I do not know who my birth parents are. I was abandoned, I believe; as a day-old baby in Glasgow. I cannot explain my DNA link to this male Joseph, other than that he must be my biological father.

I recognise the exhibit that you showed me. The polaroid MA/3 is a picture that was left with me when I was abandoned. I believe that whoever left me, left that too. I know as much as you do about the providence of that photo. The handwriting shows that one of the males is called Barnaby, and the other CJ. I cannot explain how or why it matches the photos that you found at Mr Joseph's address.

I did apply to Entwined myself, in the hope that I would find my birth parents, and although I took the test, I never actually sent it off. I do not know how they came to get my sample, and I certainly never got any communication from Entwined, to say that they had got a match. I did not arrange a meet with Mr Joseph at Bramley Wood on the 25th of April 2018, or any other day.

With regard to my neighbour, Mrs Burns, and her statement. I can confirm that she did babysit on the night of 25th April 2018, and I had intended to go to a Body Pump class. However, once I had dropped my mother off to collect her car at the Station, I realised that I was going to be late. So, I changed my plans and I went for a run at the old rec next to the allotments instead. I can only explain that the bonfire smell on my clothing, that she remembers from that night, must have come from there. I do remember changing my clothes before getting back into the car. This was because whilst I had been running, I tripped and unluckily fell in some dog muck. I had unfortunately got it on my trainers and leggings.   So, I changed into the spare clothing that I had in my gym bag. I then drove home and relieved Jeanette. I cannot provide any explanation as to why my neighbour thought she could smell petrol that night. I deny all of the allegations put before me.......and this is signed and dated Dr Michelle Jones, 15/05/2019."

Larry passes me the scrap of paper......

"I'll have a copy, please" he says.... "And you can keep the original."
"Ok, thanks for that.   I just have a few more questions."

Shirlie looks to Larry.   He gives her a reassuring smile and then rolls his eyes. *Cheeky bastard! Like he wouldn't be thorough, if he were running the show from this side of the desk!*

"OK, can I take you back to when you joined us here as an employee. What was your motivation for that?"

"No comment."

"Was it so that you had full access to the DNA Database?"

"No comment.

"Was it because you had not been initially successful in finding your parents through Entwined? Did you think that you would use the police resources, to widen your search?"

"No comment."

"Isn't it the case that when you first joined the Department, you ran your DNA on a familial search? And this searched the whole of the Database? Was that so you could help identify your parent, or family member?"

"No comment."

Shirlie shifts uncomfortably in her chair.   She is desperate to speak... *What is it you want to say??*

"Was that the plan all along? Was it revenge? Revenge for abandoning you? Or did you not get the reception that you wanted? Not the fairy-tale ending that you expected? Come on, you can tell me."

"No comment."

"We know this was planned. It had to be. The tarpaulin, the petrol, the knife…. You don't just have those items with you."

"No comment.

"What happened? Did he say something to upset you? Did he say something on the phone that you didn't like…? Is that why you lured him to his death?"

"No comment."

"We know the person who did this was forensically aware.   Would you say being the Head of Forensics, and an expert in DNA would qualify you as being forensically aware?"

"No comment."

"You see, I would. With all the "efforts" that you displayed... Staying at the lab, day and night to try and get an identity for the body. The performance, the drama. Your "act" of trying to extract the DNA. You knew there was nothing to find, because you had made sure that there was nothing identifiable of him left!"

"No comment."

"What did you do with his teeth, fingertips, and toes? Did you take his ears as well, or was that a step too far?... Come on Michelle, we are old friends, you can tell me."

"No comment."

"No wonder you seemed so stressed when I put out the facial mock-up. Were you stressed Dr Jones?"

"No comment."

Shirlie's face is getting redder and redder. She's got to crack.

"And what about his belongings? His phone, wallet, keys? What did you do with them?"

"No comment."

"Oh, and I bet you were relieved when I told you that the investigation was now with Cold Cases. Was it a big relief when I was no longer SIO? I bet you were laughing.   Thought you had got away with it…"

"No comment."

"But you hadn't, had you? Now let's talk about that key. How did you miss that? I bet you are kicking yourself. Is that why you were so obstructive, when I had asked you to authorise its Forensic Examination?"

"No comment."

"For the tape and for clarity, the key I refer to is exhibit CB/1. It's the car key for an Austin A30, Vehicle Registration RRV 339, and it was found by a dog walker at the murder scene; albeit some months after the body was discovered. It is this key that has led to my suspicion of you, and resulted in your subsequent arrest. The key is for a car that the council lifted from near the scene, and it is that car that contained the paperwork which is exhibit REC/01, detailing both yours, and the deceased DNA match confirmations from Entwined."

Larry looks at me. "Is there a question that you are trying to ask Detective Chief Inspector? It sounds to me as if you are telling a tale. In the future, maybe start it with... Once Upon a Time...."

I give him a look, and if only they could kill, he would have been struck down in an instant!

"The KEY!"

My words are through gritted teeth. He's getting right under my skin. I have got to pull myself together.   I'm so close, I just need the bitch to crack. So, taking a deep breath I form my question.

"The Key, exhibit CB/1, had you seen it prior to my request for it to be examined?"

"No comment."

"Is that why you were so obstructive? Come on, tell me about the key. Did you twig that once I had asked you to get it examined, that it might be your downfall?"

"No comment."

"Oh, come on... Is that why you buried it? You blocked its examination, citing policy and procedure?"

"Look, Detective Chief Inspector! I believe you have already asked about the key. There is no point rephrasing. We understand the question and your interest in it, but you already have the answer... No comment."

Larry is such an arse!

"Right, Ok," I say this to re-centre myself. I have lost my train of thought and I need to get it back.

"Ok, so on the night of the murder, you state that you changed your clothes because of dog muck. Do you still have these clothes?"

"No comment."

"Is it not the case that the clothes were in fact, soaked in blood and that is why you changed them?"

"No comment."

"Did you see anyone at the Rec who can back up your story? Someone in the car park perhaps? Anyone who can say that you were there, and not the 10 miles away at Bramley Wood. Killing, amputating, and cremating poor old Mr Joseph?"

"No comment."

"What did you do with the knife? Do you still have it?"

"No comment."

"Ok, so do you have anything further to add to your statement, Dr Jones? Anything at all?"

"No comment."

Shirlie looks visibly relieved, she clearly thinks that this is nearly over.

"Actually, I have just one more question. Who is Charlie Jacobs to you, and what is his link to Mr Joseph? He appears to share the same DNA as your supposed father... However, here is the confusing bit.... he also appears to be a parental match to yourself! Come on, you are the DNA expert. Help me to understand?"

Shirlie clearly knows what this means, as her eyes are as wide as dinner plates... She looks over at Larry for guidance. He shakes his head. In response to this, I can tell that rather reluctantly, she then replies, and for the final time, she says...

"No comment."
"Ok, if you have nothing further to add, interview terminated at 23:15 hours."

I then seal the master tape in their presence, and I send Rachel off to do a copy of it, as well as the prepared statement. I can't wait to send this LOB (load of bollocks) explanation to the CPS. This case may be circumstantial, but you have to admit, it's bloody compelling!

I leave Larry and Shirlie to it, and I go to sign her back into custody and out of the Interview. Bob is still on duty. He must be working a double shift... Job pissed that one!

"Ma'am, who's this for then?" Looking at the sealed CD in front of me.
"Number 9," I say. "Ok, where is she now? Are you signing her back in?"
"Yes. Can you get Billy to put her back in her cell when she's done with Larry?"

"Certainly, but it won't be Billy" he replies. "All of this must be hard for you. Wasn't she your mate? The wife of your ex, I heard." I stare at him. *What the chuff is he trying to say to me? What's his point?*

"What?"

"Well, she could have lost you this case, your reputation? She still might, you know Ma'am."

"Oh, piss off Bob! Look, I am very busy. Just get Billy, or whoever it is now to put her back, and please remember who you are addressing!"

He looks up at me grinning. He knows he's got to me.

"Oh yes, sorry Ma'am. All done. You can go and get the rest of it done now. You've not got loads of time…. The clock is ticking…."

"Yes, thank you, Bob. I do know."

I throw him a look as I exit custody. Sarky little git!

Scene Examiner Jones

I am completely shattered; I cannot believe what I have just been through. I don't even know what time it is. It's so strange not having my Fitbit on. I am so used to checking my steps, the time, my sleep patterns, and my heart rate… I can't even imagine what the beats per minute would have been today. Probably off the scale. I feel wired but my body is fit to drop.

I had had a brief chat with Larry after the "interrogation". I can tell that she really thinks that I have done this. I initially thought that this might have been some sort of hate campaign. A hangover from her and John…. But no, she really thinks she's got me. Larry's comments had made me feel a little better during his pep talk. But that's just it. It's just talk! It's alright saying "It's all circumstantial, and where's the actual evidence?" But I still got arrested and put in a cell. There was clearly enough evidence for that!

He tried to reassure me that going "no comment" was the right thing to do. I am still not sure. How could she trip me up, when I didn't do this? This still worries me... I am pleased that we did the prepared statement. At least I have provided some sort of explanation. I have to admit it, as worrying as it seems, it does all point to me.

I begin to settle down in my cell. It feels almost homely after the mental assault that I have suffered over the past couple of hours. I have also finally been for a wee. As degrading as it was, having no real privacy, it was well needed and somehow, it gave me both physical and mental relief. Seconds later and interrupting my thoughts, the heavy door swings open. I had only just wiped and flushed. "Don't you ever knock?" I snap at the silhouetted figure in the doorway. After a moment, I can see it's another young detention officer. Not Billy, he must have finished, and it's not the girl who brought me back after the interview. They have a slim physique and short hair. They look over at me, realising what I meant re knocking...

"Oh yes, um sorry, I forgot to check the wicket to see where you were."
It appears to be a male-sounding voice, although I'm not 100% sure of their gender.
"It's Ok," I say and my tone softens, whilst I rearrange my trousers. "What is it you want? I thought I got a rest period?"
"Well yes, you do, but your husband is on the phone. I thought you might want to speak to him. He's been trying to get you for hours, but you were in interview..."
"Ah ok, thank you. Where's the phone?"
"Just out here. We do normally have the facility to patch them into the cell intercom, but the one in this cell isn't working. There is a prisoner phone by the Custody Desk.   Follow me."

John

Finally, I have managed to get through to her. I had been going out of my mind with worry. How has this happened? How has she got caught up in all of this?

I sit waiting on the other end of the phone. It feels like an age before she eventually picks up. Then I hear her voice and my heart leaps.

"John, John. Is that you?"

"Yes, Baby." My voice, almost breaking. "How are you?"

"How are the girls? What have you told them? Were they ok that I didn't pick them up?"

"Yes, yes! Don't worry. Your mum is at ours. She's put them to bed. They were fine, all we said was that you had to help Aunty Jo with a case again, and that there was nothing to worry about."

"Aunty Jo, Aunty Jo! I'll never have her called that again!" She practically spits out the sentence!

I can hear the anger in her voice. Shit! I should never have said that...

"Sorry, Baby. I didn't think. Yes, yes, we won't call her that anymore. I was thinking on my feet, and it seemed the most plausible explanation. Or one that they would take without questioning... Anyway, how's it been going? How was Larry?"

"Well, I don't really know. He advised me and I did what he said to do."

"And that was?" *My breath is shallow, what did he tell her to do?*

"Well, on the whole I "no commented," and then I did a prepared statement."

"Oh ok, and how was it?"

"Bloody awful, John! How do you think it was?"

"Ok, so what did you say in the prepared statement?"

"That I didn't do it, obviously!"

"Ok great! That's great!"

"John. Do you think I did it? Hang on, is this call recorded?"

"No, Baby."

"No, Baby to what? To the call or the murder?"

"To the call...." *There is a brief silence...* "Well, did you?"

"NO!" *The word was roared down the phone.*

"Why? Did you? I have been puzzling it you know, and you had just as much opportunity and motive. Was he my father? Was he the rapist? Were you protecting me? You CAN tell me."

"No, of course not. What a thing to ask. What are you even going on about? Father? Rapist?"

"Well, someone did. And how did my test get sent off? I certainly wasn't the one that posted it!"

"What test?"

"The Entwined one. I did the DNA sample and I left it on the kitchen side. I never posted it."

"Baby, slow down. What DNA sample? I don't really get what you are saying."

(She takes an audible intake of breath, clearly irritated.)

"They have paperwork that has my name listed as having a biological link to the dead man.   He is apparently my father. I have seen the results, and supposedly according to the evidence that they have, I was meeting him on the day of his death."

"Ok, so what's his name?"

"Colin, or Charlie Joseph, something like that?"

"Ok, so what's that got to do with you?"

"Are you even listening to me?" *I can hear the irritation again in her voice...*

"Look! After Pops had died, I wanted to know who my birth parents were. I got this test and I did it, but never posted it... Anyway, somehow, they got my sample and they matched it to this Joseph chap, and he and I were apparently sent correspondence advising us of each other's existence.   A meeting between us was made on the date that they think he died. Anyway, they have identified him as the "Body in the Wood" and I am their prime suspect!"

"Ok, so they have paperwork, but no forensics, no murder weapon?"

"No, none of that, but they have a photo from our house that shows this Joseph chap."

"Well, how have they gotten that? What photo?"

"The polaroid. The one from my birth mum's diary. It says Barnaby and CJ underneath."

The penny drops...

"You see Colin Joseph, CJ. He is my rapist father, and he is the dead man."

"OK, so .... Is that what she thinks your motive is?"

"I don't know, probably. But I haven't told them about the rape, and Jo didn't mention the diary. Did they find it?"

"Not a clue and I can't check. I'm not at home."

"Why? Where are you?"

"I'm in the Front Office.   It's as far as they would let me in. Apparently, all of this is a conflict of interest. I've been put on garden leave, and my access to this building, and to any other police premises has been temporarily removed."

"Ok, well, please go home. See the girls and if you find it, put that diary somewhere safe. Jo finding it is the last thing that I need."

"Ok, no problem. One question. Who else knows about the diary and your past?"

"Well, as far as I'm aware, it's just you, me, and Mum. I don't even think that my dad knows."

"Ok, no problem.   I'll sort it. I love you, Baby. It will all be ok you know."

"How do you know?"

"I just feel it."

I can hear her voice break, as she says goodbye and the call is ended.

DCI Jo Gordon

I have finally managed to get hold of this Charlie Jacobs. I needed some sort of explanation, as to why his DNA was an exact match to the deceased. I equally needed to know the link, between him and Shirlie; parental or otherwise. Well, apparently and this explains a lot, he was a twin. He believes that Colin must have been his brother.

He explained that he and his brother were born to parents who were druggies, and that they were taken into care. He was the "younger" twin and the "runt" as he put it. Due to this, he stayed in hospital for some time after their birth. By which point, however, his brother had already been taken away, and put into the system. He, himself advised that he never heard anything else with regards to his brother... And apparently, due to some sort of issue at the records office, there was no way of tracking him down.

He said that he knew nothing of Michelle Jones, but he does know the Church at Bramley Wood. He attended there when he was a boy, and onwards through to early adulthood. He was looked after in care at the local boy's home, which was attached to that parish. By all accounts, he knew the area well. He'd moved away in his mid-20's, after having completed an Apprenticeship in Mechanical Engineering. And for the past 20 plus years, he had been living in Saudi Arabia and Dubai. He only came back to the UK, two weeks ago for a holiday. Visiting old haunts etc.

He said that his arrest was an unfortunate mistake. Caught out apparently with the "drink-drive limit". He was very apologetic, as he explained that he didn't really drink anymore. He was so used to living in "dry states".

All in all, he seemed quite a nice chap, other than when I mentioned the indecent assault that he was arrested for, back in the 1970's. He seemed to get very cagey. But then I suppose you would be. It's not really what you want to discuss, especially when it is some 40 years after the event. He had muttered something about mistaken identity.

Scene Examiner Jones

After the call from John, I was popped back into my cell. I don't even remember going to sleep. I must have just passed out, through the sheer stress and exhaustion of it all. How the hell have I got myself into this mess?

I wake up, dry-mouthed and disorientated. I then remember where I am. I still have no idea what time it is. Although, I surmise that it must be morning. The cell lights are no longer dimmed, and there are sounds of activity coming from outside of the cell door. The wicket slides open abruptly. It's Billy. He's peering through the small gap...

"Morning!" He says cheerfully. I do well to pull my blanket up over my chest. I'm not letting him feast his eyes on me this morning! "Is it?" I say with a stifled yawn. "What time is it?"
"Just gone half seven. Do you want some breakfast?"

"Yes please," I say quite eagerly. I didn't eat a thing yesterday. I couldn't, but I have just realised how hungry I am. I am so light-headed.

"Is a fry-up, ok? Well, when I say a fry-up, I mean a microwaved version of one... We don't hold a Michelin Star here!"

"Um, yes ok." It sounds disgusting, but anything is better than nothing, and I am absolutely starving.

"Tea, Coffee?"

"Coffee, please. Black, no sugar... and a water too.... My head is pounding."

"Yes! Anything else?" He says this a little indignantly. Clearly, my request for water, was a request too far.

"No, no, that's fine. Thank you, Billy."

He seems taken aback, that I know his name. He does a half-smile and then he closes the wicket, and I am then back to the silence. Well, other than my rather noisy tummy. Breakfast can't come a moment too soon.

DCI Jo Gordon

It had been a bloody long night. I wrote up my MG3, collating all the evidence and I pinged it off. I then waited and waited, and eventually, after a long telecon and a lot of persuasion from my end; the Crown Prosecution Service Lawyer finally gave me a decision.

They authorised a charge.

A charge for MURDER!

I've got her. I've only gone and done it!

Scene Examiner Jones

It is half-past eight. I know this as Billy has just deposited my coffee, water, and microwaved breakfast. He also very kindly informed me of the time. Mum and John would have been in full flow of getting the girls ready, and out of the door for school... I prayed that they wouldn't be missing me too much. Hopefully, I would be out of here soon and home...

I wolf down the breakfast. It's surprisingly good. I finish my coffee and I begin to relax a little. Settling back on the mattress, I allow my thoughts to wander whilst I wait for my next visit. I have gotten used to the various officers checking in on me, and the Inspector popping his head in for the PACE compliant reviews. In fact, it's quite comforting. It makes me feel like I've not been forgotten, and I might actually get out of here.

Anyway, Billy opens the door.

"Righty-ho. Ma'am wants you at the desk."

"Ok, I say." I swing my legs down onto the floor. *Time for me to go*, I think...

I'm walked over to the desk. It is the grey-haired Sergeant again.

"Good morning." He says with a smile. "Sleep well? Did we?"

I must look a complete mess, and I'm not really sure as to what I should reply. *Well, as Billy keeps telling me.... it's not a hotel!* I'm thinking this to myself, as I try to smooth out my hair; making some sort of effort in improving my appearance. Jo is there, she doesn't acknowledge me. She just looks directly over at the Sergeant.

"Right! Are we ready then?"

"Yes, ready when you are."

Then, I hear it, and I cannot believe what she is saying to me. My ears begin to hum. My head is pounding. Instantly my mouth becomes dry as the realisation hits me.

They are charging me.

They are charging me with MURDER!

DCI Jo Gordon

5 Months Later

The trial; it couldn't have gone any smoother. Obviously, she pleaded not guilty as I knew that she would. Even Gerald said she was hiding something. Apparently, her body language spoke absolute volumes to him. He came up with some theories, but nothing conclusive... I wish he could fully decipher her, and tell me why? What was her motive? We went down the route of revenge, at having been abandoned. But why now? And surely, she would have been angrier at her biological mother, rather than her father? After all, she carried her for 9 months and then dumped her at the pub? Maybe it had been a joint enterprise?

I still don't know what the relevance of the wood was? The twin; he knew the area from his youth, but from what I gather, Joseph had never been there before. In fact, the few people who knew of him thought he was gay, a recluse, or both. He certainly didn't have much of a presence. What did he do to her to warrant his fate?

Oh yes, and that bloody twin! He cashed in! He got paid for a piece in 'The Mirror!' A suitably sad, and pathetic image of him was splashed across the front pages. They went to town. They detailed how his chance to reconnect with his twin was robbed. Taken away by the Police's very own 'Head of Forensics!'

Yes, our Head of Forensics! ...Don't get me started... There are so many cases that have now been referred to the Criminal Cases Review Commission. Every case that she's ever been involved in. That includes the rape that she first cut her teeth on. All of them being scrutinised. Bastards! All hoping to get off on a technicality. It's a complete shit storm. Sometimes I wished I'd just let it go. I'd lose the battle, but win the war!

As expected, both John and her mother put forward their two-penneth. Advising that she had nothing to do with Entwined. Apparently, the test was posted by mistake. Irrelevant really, what did it actually prove?

I did my job. I put forward the evidence, and the Jury clearly found it compelling enough to convict. As to her reasoning why, I guess I'll never know...

Anyway, enough of all that.... Onwards and upwards. I just need to ride this storm of potential retrials.
Monroe is up for retirement in another 12 months, and I have my eye on the prize.

EPILOGUE

Josephine

It was strange. I remember the instant blackness. The nothingness after the truck hit. The blackout from the pain, and then blank. I honestly thought I was dead.

I woke up in a hospital bed. Tubes and monitors surrounding me, and the bright lights. Such bright lights. I remember the wide smiled nurse, with her really tight curly auburn hair, looking down at me. "Hello, Sleeping Beauty." She was so softly spoken. "You had us worried for a little while. I'm so glad you finally made it back. Now, what's your name?" I tried to speak but nothing really came out. I don't know how long I was out for, but my throat was raspy and dry. I eventually managed to whisper my name and address to the smiley nurse, and that was it. A couple of hours later, and Mum was at my side.

My mum looked down at me in the bed. She bent and kissed my forehead. She asked me nothing about the baby, or the accident, and no one else spoke about it either. No police Investigation into the accident. No medical staff asking about where my baby was. Surely, they would have known that I had just given birth? Wouldn't it have been obvious? No social workers wanting to know why I was so far from home, or why I had stepped out in front of the truck. Nothing. It felt surreal, almost as if it didn't happen. Had I made it up? Was it all a bad dream?

I was in hospital for a few weeks and then discharged. The Consultant's only words who signed me off were, "Well you were very lucky young lady. More care in future aye?" I couldn't really place his accent; Irish? Scottish maybe? Anyway, I nodded at him as I left, and I made my way out of the hospital with Mum. We caught a taxi to the station and took the train home. It was like

I was retracing my steps, and in a way, it was a means to erase my previous path. I was rewriting history.

On the journey home, Mum and I hardly spoke. I was tired, but that wasn't the reason why. She didn't seem to want to talk, and how would I, as an only just 16-year-old begin that type of conversation. I was still grieving; having unexpectedly lost my father, been raped, and then carried and given birth to my baby girl. I had then abandoned her, and tried and failed to kill myself. Where on earth would I start? Well, I'm sure that it won't surprise you…. but I didn't. We never had the conversation. We never spoke of it. We never spoke about any of it.

My mum, she turned her key in the lock. She opened the front door, and there it was, the familiar scent of home.

"Right then…" Mum said to me "What do you fancy for tea? I've got sausages and potatoes in. How does Toad-in-the-hole suit you?" I nodded and that was it. It was like I had never been away. We ate our dinner, I had a bath, brushed my teeth, and I went up to bed. I read a few pages of my book that was still on my nightstand, and then I went to sleep. The only deviation from my old routine, was that I did not write in my diary. I no longer had it. I had left it with her. I never wrote in a diary ever again. From that day onwards I kept all of my memories in my head. I had no need for anyone else to have access to my mind, and often the very dark thoughts that it harboured.

I went back to school the following Monday, and it was as if I had never left. In all, I had been away for over three months. No one even mentioned the fact that I'd lost weight, or looked different. Maybe they just hadn't noticed that I was pregnant in the first place. It really was as if I'd ripped out that page of my life, and the book had magically re-written itself.

Anyway, I started working really hard at school. I poured all of my energies into it; passing my O-Levels, and I even got some A-Levels as well. I totally surprised my mum. She, herself had left school aged 16. Her teacher had apparently told her parents, to not waste the guinea that they would have to pay for her maths test. Her own father, in trying to help her, had over the years completed all of her maths homework. She had sat there nodding and smiling, each time that he had checked that she had understood the process... Sadly, she did not.... Mind you, not that it really held her back. Ironically, although it was not her strong point; on leaving school she had got her first job in the local bank!

I also returned to the Church and I was welcomed with open arms. Did they really not know what had happened? I was greeted with an abundance of warm smiles and hugs. It was surreal. I vividly remember the first time that I re-attended after my "accident." I scanned and scanned that congregation. But no, I could not see him. The fear of walking in through those heavy wooden doors, and the sound of the organ being played. It was almost paralysing, and it was such a huge relief when I realised that HE was not there.

I later found out that after his apprenticeship, he'd got a job in the Middle East. He was according to everyone else, one of the church's success stories. The boy had done good. How did they not know what type of a monster he was? I didn't dwell however, what would have been the point? I had been given a second chance. Dad had clearly decided that it was not my time to join him, and so I set about making him proud.

I got my first job as a Librarian's Assistant. It was a little stuffy at times, as the Senior Librarian was very set in her ways. However, I learnt my craft from her and for that, I am very grateful. I worked my way up and finally I managed to obtain a Master's Degree in Library Science. I remember my Graduation Ceremony. I was in my late 30's by then, and Mum was elderly. She couldn't stop smiling, I had finally done something that had made her proud of me. It wasn't long after that day, that she passed on and was at peace with Dad. Poor old Dad, I bet he didn't know what had hit him. Well, not after she arrived at those pearly gates. There would be no more peace for him!

I didn't keep the house. I sold it and bought my own little place in town. It might be small, but it's mine, and the only memories that it contains are good ones. The other residents at the block, they keep to themselves. In fact, I prefer it that way. They also don't seem to mind that I maintain the garden. I don't think I have ever seen anyone else out there. It's my sanctuary and it's where I do most of my thinking.

It was back in February, three or four years ago, or maybe longer when I was doing a winter tidy up. The weather had been really rather mild, and the spring bulbs were coming up early, so I went to clear away the last of the fallen leaves on the beds. It was then that she popped into my head.

"My daughter."

Over the years I had not thought much about her. It wasn't that I didn't want to. It was just that I had never spoken of her. I was worried that if I even so much as considered her; a simple rogue thought for example. It would open up Pandora's Box, and that would be me done for.

Anyway, curiosity got the better of me, and whilst I was at work, I googled her. Well, not her as such. I googled the date that I let her go, and the name and the location of the pub. Then, low and behold... I found her. It was so easy with my open-source research skills. Someone had done a piece in a Science Journal about this successful DNA professor, whose actual origins were unknown. I knew as soon as I saw her image, looking back at me from the laptop screen. I knew that she was my daughter, and I was delighted by what I read about her. I burst with pride knowing that she was a success. I didn't expect to feel like that. It must have been instinct, but I was grinning from ear to ear, and I was desperate to know more about her. I also felt validated. I had made the right decision all those years ago. My teenage-self had done the right thing.

It didn't take long for me to track her down. She was working at the university in town. The town that all those years ago, I had tried so hard to get her away from. Fate really is a funny thing. She had ended up where she began.

That night when I said goodbye. I had left her North of the border. In a different country and she'd still found herself back here.

When I first saw her in the University Carpark, I was so excited, I was fit to burst. I wanted to run straight to her, and to tell her who I was, but something stopped me. I didn't know what it was... I considered that it might have been the shame, that I had abandoned her, and or the fear that she might actually reject me? I also had had a lifetime of guilt, due to my decision of leaving my diary with her that night. I wondered if she had cracked the code? Did she know her true origins? It was only later on in life, that I realised just how cruel I'd actually been. She was a victim and an innocent in all of this, as was I. She did not need to know that kind of pain. To discover that she was not born out of love. The often-presumed product of a foolish teenage fling. No, she was the result of a cruel and violent act. Her daddy; he was a rapist. I truly hoped that she had not discovered the truth. However, and after a while of getting to know her, I feared that she already knew. When I say getting to know her, I don't mean that we sat in a café with a cuppa and a slice of cake. Both of us casually chatting, and learning about each other's lives. No, I meant I watched her. From the shadows, I got to know my daughter, her family, and her routines.

It was never actually my intention to follow, or to stalk her. I just wanted to know who she was, and where she lived. I had so many questions. Was she married? Was I a grandma? I needed to know that she was happy. And I needed to know that, without any chance of rejection, or reproach. She became my project.

When I first followed her home, I was so happy to see that she had done well for herself. She lived on a lovely tree-lined street, no more than a 30-minute drive from my own home. Her house was double fronted and set back from the road. It was perfect. That very first night I sat in my car and just watched from afar.

It was a busy house, lots of comings and goings. She'd arrived home, and an older female opened the door to her. She embraced my daughter. A friend? Nanny? I wasn't sure of the relationship. Adoptive Mother perhaps? I just didn't know. What I was sure of however, was that I was definitely a grandma. Two little girls had greeted their mother, (my daughter) at the door. Their resemblance to me as a child, even from a distance, was uncanny. I sat in the car and watched the older female leave; again, kissing and hugging at the door. Who was she? It didn't really matter. I knew that I'd find out in due course. Anyway, they were clearly close.

I sat for a little longer, and I saw a large 4x4 type car arrive, it parked up on the driveway. I couldn't quite make out their facial features, but the driver's physique was athletic. He removed a big black kitbag from the car and he let himself into the house with a key. I worked out that he must be my son-in-law.

I was so excited. Once more I had a family. You see; after Mum had died, I found that I had become really lonely. Don't get me wrong, I had colleagues at work, and I had neighbours. But no one that I could call my own. A tear welled up. I knew I had to tell her who I was. But not that night. That night, I was pleased that I had learnt a bit more about her, and that she was settled. I drove home happy and contented. I had found her. I was full of hope.

***

Watching her, became my hobby. Dependant on what shift I was on at the library; I would catch her either before or after work. I would see her pick up the girls from school. The love and the embraces that she gave to those children, were what I longed to show and give to her myself.

My daughter was very busy.   She was always going here and there. She kept fit, just like me.   I'd often trail her to the gym, or see her pop out from work. She'd regularly go running whilst on her lunch break. She seemed like she really had it together, it was all I could have hoped for.

It was only after numerous months of watching her, that I noticed that her usual clockwork routine, suddenly deviated.   I'd had an unexpected change of shift, and I was working on the Saturday, instead of the Monday.   I was at a loose end, so I thought that I would go and check on her.

She left work daily, roughly around the same time. I noted that this only really changed, if she were picking up the girls. So, on this particular day, rather than head straight home, she took a detour. Intrigued by this, I of course followed her.

She drove to a quiet street. She parked up, and went into the house opposite. I had watched her as she buzzed an intercom to be let in to the address. I could see that there was a list of names on the door. However, from my location, I couldn't make out what any of them said. I sat in my car and waited for her to come out. After turning the radio on, I began to groove to some classic tunes from my youth. Duran Duran, Go West. They were all being belted out. In fact, I was so engrossed in the 1980's, and singing at the top of my voice, that I thought I'd missed her. Panicking, I took a quick glance in the rear-view mirror, and thankfully I spotted that her car was still there.

It took an age, but she finally reappeared from the building. She crossed the road, heading back towards her car. I could see from her body language that she seemed sad. Although I wasn't entirely sure. Was she crying? What had happened in there?

I let her drive away, and I got out of my car and walked the few yards across the street, and over to the building. I looked at the names on the intercom. A Solicitors, an Accountants, and a Counsellor. All of them housed in this old Victorian Building, on a quiet residential street. Who was she meeting? I had to know.

I watched her for the rest of the week (my shifts allowing, of course...) but she didn't go back. I wanted to see if it was a one-off, but Mondays were my regular workdays.

It had worried me all weekend, so the following Monday, I took a sickie. I had to see if she went back to the address again. Was this a part of her life that I'd missed because of my Monday commitment at the library?

Sure enough, after work rather than head straight home, she went back to the old Victorian building. Again, she was there for approximately an hour, and then she left. Once more, on leaving she looked troubled. What was it? Was she in debt? Did she need legal advice? Was she getting a divorce? Was my son-in-law playing away? Had she caught him? I was panicking, and I had so many questions. I knew I needed to help her, but how?

It then dawned on me. Maybe I'd be able to tell what help she was getting, by looking at the opening hours of the firms. It took no more than sixty seconds on Google, for me to discover that my daughter was seeing a therapist. As both the Accountants and the Solicitors firms, listed their opening hours as 09:00 - 17:00 hours.

The counselling service however, was open from midday until 20:00 hours...

My daughter didn't actually arrive at the address until after five... so I had my answer, and it hit me like a brick. She knew. She must do, and she clearly needed help in processing it. I felt absolutely wretched.

I had difficulty sleeping after that day. It was all I could think about. I knew that her troubles were all my fault. If only I had taken the diary and put it in the bin, as I had done with her hospital band. She would never have known, and she wouldn't be needing the services of a therapist. Ignorance is bliss. Her life; from what I had observed so far, was pretty much idyllic. It was clear to me that it could only be this shadow from her past, that was causing her such concern. As her mother, I was desperate to help. I wanted to take her pain away.

For months and months, I just watched. I tried to pluck up the courage to approach her, but I couldn't. I just didn't know how. But then, one day her routine just changed. She stopped coming to work. Initially, I considered that she had just changed her car, but a quick drive past her house proved that she hadn't ... It was still parked up on the drive. Maybe she was on holiday or ill? I left it a day or so, but she didn't seem to go back in.

Also, at around the same time, I had taken on some extra responsibilities at the library, and I had been very busy with a number of new initiatives. I hadn't had the time, nor the flexibility to check on her. I hoped her reason for not being at the University was nothing serious, as my current workload had reduced my ability to keep a track of her activities.

Over a period of two weeks, the not knowing had really started to get to me. My rational mind told me that she was just on holiday... however the constant worry had really affected my sleep.

One morning I was up again with the larks, so I decided to drive past her address. Fate clearly felt it would intervene, and so as luck would have it, I saw that she was just leaving. I was happy to see that she was ok, but also intrigued as to where she was off to at such an early hour. It wasn't even seven o'clock yet! I followed her, and to my confusion, she drove straight to the Police Station. I couldn't work it out. Why was she there? She parked up, and was stood chatting to this blonde, brash looking woman. They seemed to know each other, and appeared to be friends, or at the very least good colleagues. She got her laptop out from the boot of her car, and suddenly it dawned on me. She'd changed jobs. I was so relieved.

Her new routine, was more and more difficult to track once she had started with the Police. I wasn't entirely

sure what she was doing for them. It must have been a
good job, as she worked long hours. It was clearly
important, but I was finding it hard keeping tabs.
Thankfully however, she always parked in the same
spot, so I could always tell if she were there or not.

One morning, back in late January I woke up, and I
decided that today was the day. I had been pondering it
for ages. I was going to introduce myself.

It was a bright crisp morning, and it just felt right. The
sun was streaming in through the window. I jumped
out of my bed; I felt the warmth inside my heart. Today
was the day that I was going to finally meet my
daughter.

I had a full breakfast and I got dressed in my best
trouser suit. I also straightened my hair, and I put some
makeup on. Looking in the mirror, I admired my

reflection. I looked presentable. I wanted to look like someone that she would want to get to know.

My stomach was full of butterflies. My mouth was dry, but I knew it was now or never. I just prayed that she wasn't at work. I had managed to work out some sort of pattern to her days, and I was pretty sure that today she was off. I got into my car and I headed over to her address. I made it in no time at all. Every light was on green. Everything was in my favour. It was a good omen; I was sure of it. I parked up, and I made my way over to the little wrought iron garden gate. I couldn't see her car but I was there now, and I needed to at least see if she was home.

My thoughts fully focused on my task, meant that I hadn't noticed that there was someone over to the left of me. He made me jump. Once I had taken him into view. I saw that he was a grey-haired man, dressed in red with a satchel....

"Morning!" He said with a jovial sing to his voice. "Oh, good morning," I said back to him, a little startled. I hadn't factored having to speak to anyone else, and it threw me a little. He was holding something in his hand, and once I had regained my focus, I realised he was the Postman. Unsurprisingly, he was holding a bundle of letters. "Blimey!" He said. "Well... I can tell you are related. What are you, sisters?" He said this with a cheeky grin. I wasn't sure if he was being kind, sarcastic, or ironic. I smiled back at him in any case, and then before I knew what I was saying, I replied "I'm her aunt."

"Ah lovely, just over for a visit then? Nice. Well ...you can save my legs then." ... And at that, he shoved the bundle of letters that he had in his hand into mine, and he was off down the street. Well... I can't go back on it now; I've got to go up to the house, even if it's just to deliver the letters. At this, I glanced down, and I recognised a logo on the uppermost envelope. It was addressed to her and it was from Entwined. I knew exactly what company they were, and what they did. Oh, my goodness. I could feel my face flushing. She's been looking for me. I was absolutely elated.

I ran up the path, and I knocked on her door but nothing happened. No one came to answer it. No one was there. I was just about to post all the letters through the door, when I decided to keep hold of the Entwined one. I knew that I wasn't on their database, so rather than dash her hopes with this letter, which would clearly say no match found. I took it home with me.

It was only once I was sat at my kitchen table, with a cuppa and my favourite rich tea biscuit, that I thought I'd better open it. Well … it was of no use to her. I was already found, and it was only a matter of time before I had managed to introduce myself to her.

I ripped open the envelope, and I could not believe my eyes. Anger instantly rose up within me. I read it and read it again. The dirty old bastard! The man who had raped me was searching for MY daughter! I was shaking with rage. In black and white, I had his full name, address, and contact number. I didn't know what I was going to do, but I knew that he was never going to meet her. He was never going to hurt me, or anyone else again.

***

I did what I did. I had no choice…. It really was the only way, and I had made peace with it. He was dead. It was finally over.

***

I had obviously checked the news feeds hourly at first. Local twitter groups, and anything that might say that he'd been found, but there was nothing. But then, it happened. The media storm.

I realised that unfortunately, she had been drawn into it. She was working long hours, and she was always, it seemed with that brash blonde woman. The one that I'd seen her with, on that first day when I realised that she'd changed jobs. Lately however, anytime that I saw them together, their interactions outside of the building, seemed fraught and less familiar. She also looked really unwell. She had lost a load of weight, and I could see the anxiety. It was written all over her face. It was killing me not to introduce myself, but I knew that right now, it would be too risky. I needed all of this to blow over. Only then, could I tell her that I had saved her. She was safe, and she would never need to worry ever again.

Except, that day never came. For all my careful, and forensic planning, somehow, they managed to identify him. For weeks on end, I had gone through every single Forensic Crime Book that I could get my hands on. I never officially borrowed them from the library, but I devoured each one, from cover to cover. I needed to know how to get away with this. I could not be punished again. I had had a lifelong punishment, and I had finally found my freedom and I was never going back to before.

I could not believe what I was reading, and I was physically sick when I saw the news. It was a ticker-tape scrolling at the bottom of the screen. 'BREAKING NEWS' it said. It was almost immediate. I had a watery taste in my mouth, followed by bile…. They had arrested and charged her. How? What evidence did they have? I had done this; it was all my fault and she was being punished for it. I wanted to drive straight there and to tell them that they had got it wrong. I didn't though, I knew that wasn't the solution, as she would still be lost to me. I still would not get to hold her, as I would be locked up in her place. Even beyond the grave, he managed to hurt me. My only hope was that the Jury would look at the evidence, or lack of, and realise that SHE HAD NOT DONE THIS, and they would acquit her.

It took months for the trial to be heard at court. I felt terrible. I lost so much weight. So much so, that at work, colleagues asked if I were ill. I made up some story about IBS. I wish I'd used another ailment, as Anne then bombarded me with online articles, about what I should and should not be eating. She meant well, but for goodness' sake!

From the back row of the Public Gallery. I listened intently as the Foreman of the Jury delivered the verdict…. "GUILTY."

I looked over at her. She was gaunt. I could see that all this had taken its toll, and it was all my fault. She didn't even look up. She never made eye contact with anyone.

I wanted to shout out and tell her, tell all of them. It was me! But I couldn't! I couldn't let him punish me again.

There needed to be another way.

After that day in court, my sole purpose was researching ways of getting her acquitted-on appeal. I read every article that I could find. Everything seemed to hinge on the introduction of new evidence. I had that new evidence, but I had to play this right.

I was just putting together my appeal case, the one that I had decided to send to my daughter's husband. When I saw HIM….

There was a tabloid upturned on my desk. It was 'The Mirror', and not a paper that I would ever read. I wasn't entirely sure how it got where it did. However, on the front page, and looking back at me was HIM! Then, I read the headline. ROBBED OF MEETING TWIN BROTHER, DUE TO BRUTAL MURDER. Shit! As I read on, I realised the crippling truth. That day, he wasn't lying. It really wasn't him. He didn't do that terrible thing that had haunted me all these years. It was his twin.

I had unfortunately killed an innocent man.

The realisation of what I had done was too much. I began to shake. My chest tightened, and I could hardly breathe. All this had been for nothing. He was still a stain on this earth…. Then I'm not sure what happened next, but I must have blacked out.

I awoke to a paramedic trying to bring me round. "Hello, hello, can you hear me, open your eyes". I did as I was commanded, and I opened them. I wished that I had done that all those months ago, and seen the truth. I was so clouded in rage that "HE" was trying to contact her. I missed the fact that actually, it might not have been him. The science, it was so conclusive...but of course, identical twins share the same DNA.

The Paramedic was a youngish lad. "Are you ok there? You gave your colleagues quite a scare. It was a good job that we were only across the street. They called me over, just as I was getting a pasty for my lunch from Greggs. Do you know what happened?" I shake my head. "Your vitals seem ok; do you want to come with us? I don't think there is anything to worry about, but it might be nice to get checked over?"
"No, thank you" I reply. "I feel fine. I clearly just needed a rest." He smiles.
"Ok, if you are sure. Sorry, but do you mind signing this paperwork, just to say that you don't wish to go to hospital... We've got to cover our backs these days!?"
"No problem." I say whilst I put my pen to paper.

I still feel a bit off, but I know that I have got things to do. I've not a minute to waste. I'm told to go home and rest, and I don't argue. I gather my things and I make my way home. I catch the bus, leaving the car. After my episode, I still don't feel up to driving.

Once I'm home, I make myself a cuppa, and pull out a pen and some paper from the dresser drawer. I then start to write. It is well into the evening, and it is dark by the time I am finished.   I am tired, and now I have a crippling headache. I take two paracetamol. Exhausted; I fall asleep in the chair.

I awake the next morning to the sunlight shining in through the window. I look down at the scribbled pages on the floor to the left of me. I'm not sure what I'd call it. Confession? Memoir? It tells my story, detailing my rapist's brother's demise, and my complete and utter remorse.

I pick it up and go to the kitchen, placing it carefully on the table. I then pour myself an orange juice, and I head to the bathroom for a shower.

Afterwards, I feel refreshed. I emerge from the bedroom, dressed in a black hoodie and jogging bottoms. I pack a bag with some essentials, and then I head to the shed and I gather up the key pieces of evidence, that will prove my daughter's innocence.

I then leave the house and head straight to the Police Station. It's still early as I walk into the Front Office. There is a young officer with his feet up on the desk. He is clearly having a doze. I clear my throat to get his attention. Shocked, he sits bolt upright.

"Sorry." He says. "I must have dozed off. Night shift." He says this, I think as some sort of explanation... I nod and I pass him the carrier bag that I have with me. "What's this then?" He says.

"It's for your Boss. The one who dealt with the "Body in the Wood" case. Is she in the office yet?" I enquire.

Clearly, he is still half asleep, but he replies. "Um yes….

She might be… keeps long hours, does Ma'am.

Although, I doubt that she has sneaked in past me. It's unlikely, you see, as I'm sure she would have definitely bollocked me for falling asleep…. I'll check, back in a jiffy."

Superintendent Jo Gordon

I am getting used to this grand office being mine. I couldn't believe it when Monroe finally retired. That job was the making of me, and the reason that I got this promotion. I'm still getting accustomed to the title of "Superintendent" …. Sounds great, doesn't it!!

There is a knock on the door. "Come in" I say.

The heavy door opens, and there is the young officer who I saw asleep at the front desk.

"Ah good morning! Finally woken up, have we?" Sheepishly, he looks over at me. "Um… yes, Ma'am …. Sorry about that. I've got a young baby."
"Yes, I'm well aware of your home circumstances. I'm all-knowing and all-seeing. You had better watch out!"
…*The Superintendent taps the side of her nose as she says this…*. "I didn't get to these heady heights without

knowing what my flock is up to...." *She then winks at him as she is clearly in a good mood*.... "And seeing as nobody was waiting this morning, I let it go.... now.... What do you want? If it's to take my coffee order, I thank you.... White without!"

"Well... Ma'am. No, not coffee." *He says sounding flustered. He was a little taken back by the Superintendent's joviality for this time in the morning. Was she flirting with him?*... Clearing his throat, he continues....

"There is a female downstairs.   She gave me this and asked me to pass it on to you."

"Has she now... Well ... What is it? Come in, come!" I say this impatiently.

"Um... I'm not really sure, Ma'am." He says this with a poorly stifled yawn.

"Oh, give it here... hopefully it's not anthrax!" I say this jokingly, as I reach over and grab it out of his hand. I look inside, and I can see a mobile phone, what looks like a polaroid photo, and something wrapped up.

Pulling on a pair of latex gloves, I reach inside.

Wrapped up in a carrier bag is a bloodied knife….

"Shit, what is this stuff? What exactly did she say when she gave this stuff to you?"

My heart is starting to race, I see straight away that the photo is the same as I have in the property store. Although, there is no writing on this one.

"She just told me to give it to my boss. The one who dealt with the Body in the Wood."

"Shit! …. And is she still there? Go down and take her to an interview room and if she refuses; arrest her!"

"What Ma'am, arrest her? What… What for?"

"I don't know yet…. but just don't let her go… Quickly, chop, chop!" (*The young officer is slow to react*) …

"Bugger me! … Get out of my way, I'll go and do it myself!"

I rush past the streak of piss that is stood in my doorway, and I'm straight down the stairs. I must have looked like a vaulting gazelle trying its utmost to avoid being someone's prey; however, in this scenario I was definitely the Lioness.

I get to the Front Office. It is empty. I immediately rush out to the carpark and the street beyond. Again, empty. She has vanished into thin air. I put it out on the radio, but with the limited description, and with no direction of travel, there is as expected, the almost immediate response of "… area search, no trace, Ma'am."

Walking back into my office. I am still holding the paperwork that came with the phone, knife, and photo. I read it, and as the realisation hits; sick rises up, and into my mouth. I have made the biggest mistake of both my life and career.

Josephine

Walking out and into the fresh air, I feel content. I have finally told the Police; I have confessed to the murder. I now know how it feels to have a "weight off your mind". It's not how I imagined it, but soon my baby girl will be freed, and HE will finally be dealt with.

HE will be punished for what he did to me, and this time, I will get it right.

Josephine disappears into the morning sunshine, a black holdall slung over her shoulder, and a spring in her step.

THE END.

Follow Shelley and Josephine's story in the next instalment of the Rachel Cooper Series… Get your copy of **HUNTED** today!

Available to purchase on Amazon as a paperback or as a download from the Kindle Store.

A note from the author...

Thank you so much for taking the time to read my book. I really appreciate your support.

If you liked what you read, or even if you didn't, please feel free to leave me some constructive feedback.

If you did enjoy this however, and want to read another book written by me.... why not try the next book in the Rachel Cooper Series? All three books are available to download as e-books on Kindle or as paperback editions on Amazon.

Body in the Wood, Hunted & Absolution.

If you want to keep up to date with my latest projects, or you just want to know more about me, why not follow me on Amazon, or visit my website:

www.kecullenwriter.co.uk

Printed in Great Britain
by Amazon

84507778R00205